Show Me No Mercy

Anita L. Roseboro

The Cambry Group
Hickory, North Carolina
Anita L. Roseboro

This is a work of fiction. Names, characters, places and incidents are products of the author's imagination or are used fictitiously and are not to be construed as real. Any resemblance to actual events, locales, organizations, or persons, living or dead, is entirely coincidental.

Show Me No Mercy by Anita L Roseboro
The Cambry Group
Copyright 2018

Trade Paperback: 978-1-7321300-0-5
E-book: 978-1-7321300-3-6

Cover designed by: J.L. Woodson www.jlwoodson.com
Interior design by: Lissa Woodson www.naleighnakai.com
Cover Image: Woodson Creative Studio www.woodsoncreativestudio.com

Printed in the United States of America

Show Me No Mercy

Dedication

To Louise Carson Roseboro; I miss you dearly, mom.

Anita L. Roseboro

Acknowledgements

All glory and honor belong to God, my Father for the gift and the ability to put words together and spin a story.

Brian and Cameron, my sons: You two are the reasons I never give up. In order to prove that you can accomplish anything you set your mind to, I have continued this journey so that you never let go of your dreams. Thanks for tolerating my lack of attention, and my never-ending questions. Also, thanks for promoting my book to all your friends. I love you guys and appreciate you. I am so proud of the men you have become.

Charles and Kim, my brother and sister-in-love: Thanks for the early reads of my story. The pre-edit to the edit. Thanks for the endless encouragement in pursuing my dreams. Much love to both of you.

Victoria Christopher Murray: Thank you so much for your Writing Workshop, and for Boot Camp. Your belief in my writing helped start the journey. Love you much.

Pastor Ron and Pastor Katie: For always being there, even when I didn't know you were pulling for me. Thanks for covering me in prayers. Thank you for the help with the Pastors portion of the book.

Victoria Roberts, my encourager: You have encouraged me and called me to the carpet so much. Thanks for renewing my faith and building me up. Thanks for keeping me grounded in the Word and for being my biggest cheerleader.

Sister Scribes: I thank you for the encouragement. I'm thankful for each of you and your own individual talents. God has purposed each of us for something different with all our unique stories slotted for this time. Pursue your destinies ladies.

Bishop Don and Pastor Helen: Thank you for covering me in prayer and all the encouraging words. Thank you for accepting me.

Priscilla Jackson, Debra Mitchell, Christine Pauls, Michelle Rayford—my Betas, and Mo Sytsma and J. L. Campbell, line editors: You ladies are remarkable. Each one packs their own strength and powers. Together you have worked to bring this story to fruition. Love you ladies.

Lisa Watson, author, editor: You showed up in the 9th inning and hit it out of the park. Thanks for all your additions and timely creativity to tie up all the loose ends

Naleighna Kai, author, developmental editor, friend: I wish I could give to you everything you've given me. Your selflessness can't even be measured. You give until it hurts, literally. Your knowledge and love of the literary process is unmatched. I don't take this journey with you for granted. I wouldn't even be here without you. For your tribe you give 200%. I'm grateful that God saw fit to put you in position just when I needed you. Thanks for pushing me and the swift kick in the hind parts when I need it. You slay. I want to be you when I grow up. J.L. Woodson; You are a graphic designing beast!!!!!

To the readers: I appreciate you more than you know. Thanks for purchasing my work and I look forward to your feedback.

If I forgot anyone please charge it to my head and not my heart.

Thank you everyone.
Anita L. Roseboro

Anita Roseboro's debut novel was amazing. Talented writing, deep emotion, and a heavy story line made me want to finish to find out how Casey goes on to deal with her trauma at the hands of someone she should have been able to trust. There's nothing easy about the subject matter-- in fact, I was angry, but those intense emotions I felt, made me sure that this author has a gift that I can't wait to continue to explore. Bravo!"

Prologue

"The police will catch the monster who did this," the red-haired nurse said, giving Casey a reassuring glance.

Casey shifted, trying to ignore the pain, her vision blurred with unshed tears as she whispered, "They won't have to look far. He's my husband."

Chapter 1

Cedar Crest Inn
Asheville, NC

Fueled by adrenaline, Casey staggered out of the bedroom, and inched down the stairs to the main lobby. She almost made it to the door when a woman's voice stopped her.

"Wait, are you okay?"

Casey looked over her shoulder. The silver-haired hostess, Mrs. Harper, was standing near the front desk holding a cup of tea; worry etched in the lines across her face. "Can I help you?"

"Where's the hospital?" Casey asked, unable to keep the tremors from her voice.

"About a mile down the road."

Casey nodded and moved toward the door.

"You didn't say no or stop. How is it rape?" he'd said.

"Honey, it's snowing outside," Mrs. Harper warned, causing Casey to glance at her as she placed the cup on the counter and rounded the desk. "You can't go out in just a comforter and no shoes. Let me help you."

"No," Casey protested recoiling. The last thing she wanted was for this woman, who'd been so kind since they arrived, to know what her husband had done. "I'm fine," she lied, knowing that was far from the truth.

"You're my wife ... I love you," he said. "How can you think I'd rape you?"

She tipped out of the inn's front door. Her only protection from the freezing temperature was the tan comforter draped around her body. She didn't feel the snow on her bare feet and somehow managed to coordinate her limbs enough to make it to the car. Casey unlocked the door and tried to slide behind the wheel. Nothing could have prepared her for the searing pain that hit when she attempted to sit down. Crying out, she immediately shifted her weight until she was lying on her side across the seat.

Casey tried to summon the strength to get herself to safety, but the adrenaline that had carried her to this point was dwindling fast. She had to get out before he came after her.

A knock on the window made every cell in her body tense, thinking it could be Terrence. She instantly regretted the quick movement.

"Casey," Mrs. Harper called out, opening the door slowly. "You're in no condition to drive. Please, let me take you to the hospital."

At this point, she didn't have enough energy to fight, so she merely allowed the older woman to help her into the back seat before they drove away.

Taking shallow breaths, Casey tried to keep calm, but her husband's words echoed in her head and the emotional pain that struck her heart outweighed any physical pain.

"It was an accident ..."

"I never meant to hurt you ..."

* * *

When they arrived, Mrs. Harper guided Casey through the emergency room doors and to the patient registration desk. A security officer walked behind them, warning, "your car can't stay in the entrance zone."

"I'll be right back," Mrs. Harper said, turning to follow the burly man back in the direction they came.

"No, I'm here now," Casey protested. "You go on back to the Inn. I'll be alright."

Mrs. Harper moved the car and returned the keys to Casey. "I'll catch a taxi back to the Inn."

"Ma'am, what's the nature of your emergency?" a stone-faced intake nurse asked.

Casey chewed the inside of her jaw, tamping down an instant reply. She pulled the tan comforter tighter around her trembling body trying to ignore the curious stares of onlookers in the waiting room. A flamboyantly dressed woman with strawberry blonde hair eyed her carefully from a few feet away, while a couple holding a squirming toddler stared openly. No surprise when all of them inched back to give Casey some space.

"Wait … what did I do wrong?"

Her body, torn in a place where she warned him that she would never receive him, was racked with pain so severe that every step was pure agony. Blood had saturated the bottom half of the soft material wrapped around her body, but the worker had not looked up to gauge the situation. Instead, she had kept her sky-blue eyes focused on the computer while sliding a clipboard over the counter. What angered Casey the most was that the woman operated by habit, oblivious to the fact that she was the first point of contact for those coming into the hospital after suffering various injuries.

"Fill out this paperwork front and back," she said dryly. "Return it to me when you finish."

Feeling dismissed, Casey slid the clipboard from the ledge and cautiously maneuvered past those who averted their gazes. After a few minutes of being unable to find any stable position where the pain was not a constant enemy, or without the memory of why she was in this current state flashing in her mind, she realized standing at the counter would be best.

"Baby, believe me … it was an accident."

The worker gestured in Casey's direction while speaking with another much taller woman on her right, but Casey was too far away to hear the conversation. She handed the clipboard over and watched as the woman keyed some information into a computer while the tall one hovered over her shoulder.

Infuriated by the disrespect, Casey let loose with, "Not once have you looked up from that screen to make eye contact with any of the people who are here."

Suddenly, a spike of tension hit the waiting room. Once again, all eyes focused on Casey.

"We're decent people," Casey said as another nurse snapped to attention and moved closer. "People with real situations; who need just a little compassion. Obviously, you've been at this job so long that you're desensitized to the human aspect of your position." She leaned in, bracing against the counter so she could stay upright. "After everything I've been through this morning, having to deal with your callous attitude has been far more degrading."

When the woman still had not given her eye contact, Casey snapped, "Look at me."

Finally, she had the woman's full attention. "What's the nature of your emergency?"

Casey simply stared at her, waiting until the nurse's gaze lowered, doing a thorough onceover this time. Her blue eyes widened in shock. "You could've said that you've been raped," she whispered, and actually had the nerve to sound annoyed.

"It wasn't just rape," Casey said in a low voice. "It was something so despicable that I can't even say it out loud. The fact that I'm here should've been important enough no matter what happened to me." She finished in a voice loud enough for others to hear.

Grumbles of agreement from the waiting patients echoed behind Casey. Some even applauded.

The nurse flinched, then mumbled something to the other nurse that Casey could not quite catch. A more matronly woman walked over, placed a hand on the intake nurse's shoulder and said, "Why don't you take a break, Brenda. We'll talk later."

Brenda stood, grimaced, directed a stony gaze at Casey and said, "I apologize for your inconvenience," before trudging down a hallway that led to a double set of wooden doors.

"My name's Olivia," the older nurse offered, touching Casey's elbow. "I'll take over from here." Chestnut eyes, filled with warmth, flickered over Casey's ill-clad form as she added, "The police will catch the monster who did this."

"I'm sorry. I never meant for that to happen."

Casey's vision blurred with unshed tears as she whispered, "They won't have to look far. It's my husband."

Chapter 2

Ten minutes later, Casey was lying on her side on the cold examining table as Olivia and the doctor attended to her. When Olivia said, "the monster that did this," her mind flipped back to their suite at the inn. Monster was never a word she had associated with her husband.

"You raped me."

"Wait. What? No…" Terrence cried, struggling to get out of her reach, then he gasped and looked down. "I didn't mean to do that."

His flesh twisted in Casey's vice-like grip like a dried dishrag after months of use. The more he screamed, the harder she tried to force all the feeling from his flaccid member. Nothing else, no other life should come from his shady gene pool.

What he'd done was incomprehensible. The images of him slamming into a place she considered off-limits, flashed with the same cadence as the continued throbbing in her body. She could barely move. She could barely part her lips to speak.

Guilt crept in. The Christian Woman's Guild warned that good Christian woman did not indulge in any sex outside of the missionary position.

Filthy. That one word summed up her feelings, but still didn't adequately describe the aftermath of such an unexpected ordeal. Anniversary. Romantic weekend, Rape. One of those words was not like the others.

Still lying near the edge of the examining table that had seen its share of wounded, bruised, and dying patients, she was transfixed by the realization that her marriage, such as it had been, was over.

Terrence seemed to have no regard for the fact that in the midst of his actions she couldn't even form the words "no" or "stop." The thought only increased her anger as she remembered how she tried to free herself.

He had been oblivious to her end of the experience until she grabbed his groin, halting his drive to completion and refused to release him. This time, she was the one ignoring pleas loud enough to bring the owners of the Cedar Crest Inn to their door.

This wasn't the anniversary weekend she had imagined. From the moment she won the free night at the inn through a raffle for a coworker's son, she had planned everything; every detail. It would take three-and-a-half-hours to drive to the four-story Victorian Inn after leaving their jobs in Columbia, South Carolina. She even went so far as adding an extra night and had the owners leave some massage oil, a fruit tray, chocolate, vanilla scented candles, and a chilled bottle of Stella Rosa Moscato in their suite. She'd also brought along a little lubricant to ease things since she'd experienced unusual dryness after the last child. The kind of romantic getaway a couple with a growing family needed.

Their three-month-old son, TJ, and seven-year-old daughter, Skye, had taken up so much of her time and attention that getting away from her patients, the kids, and her parents was not only supposed to be a special celebration for them, but also a much-needed reprieve for her.

Terrance had been a godsend every step of the way from the moment she decided to become a psychiatrist to the time she made the choice to delay having the children he had wanted. He supported her all the way down the line, even when she stayed home longer than planned after the first child.

So, this … was totally unexpected. Terrance was a family man through and through, more than what he'd witnessed in his own family. He had always promised to be there for her, and the children and he'd kept his word and never asked for much in return.

The echoes of her husband's loud cries brought her back to the present. The energy that raced through her body and battled with the ache that was taking forever to subside had put her in fight mode. Every martial arts move she had learned for situations where a stranger could attack had flashed in her mind. None of it had helped when it counted. Not a single grappling technique or counter-attack came to mind when her husband had her face down in the pillows and propped up in the most vulnerable position possible.

"I said I never wanted this, but you didn't listen," she said through her teeth. "Now you want me to stop because you're in pain? What about my pain?"

She had never wanted sex that way and had expressed that fact, first, when a request passed his lips a year after Skye was born. The second time came after they'd joined a church that took a hard line when it came to men being head of the household. Men were to be in total control of their family's finances, decisions, and every aspect of their lives, including the bedroom. While the pastor was preaching wives submit, the church mothers were preaching missionary position, and that anything else was an abomination. Now, Casey wondered if this had been a part of Terrence's angle all along. If so, how naïve she'd been. And how her husband had changed.

An hour ago, she had taken a deep breath before releasing Terrence from that death grip in which she held him. He had inched backward, putting distance between them, then collapsed onto the bed, twisting on the rumpled sheets, holding himself and whimpering like a puppy, while trying to get a few apologies in between.

Casey stumbled off the bed, her voice dripping with disdain as she said, "You chose to show me no mercy. Now you know how it feels."

Chapter 3

Cedar Crest Inn
Honeymoon Suite

Terrence's groin still pulsated with an agonizing ache that escalated every time he tried to move. He didn't have the strength to summon an ambulance for his wife. He had wanted to run after her, but with minimal mobility from her assault, he couldn't manage. Instead, he yelled, "Casey, it was a mistake," hoping she heard him.

Rape? How could she think he'd meant to hurt her in that way? They were having sex, good sex. He slipped and … that's all. He was so close to an orgasm, it didn't dawn on him that not only was she not enjoying his efforts, but she had, in fact, felt violated. He *never* intended that. Ever. He had loved Casey from the moment he laid eyes on her at new student orientation, on the campus of UNC-Asheville, and he would love her still. It pained him that she felt he was capable of something so heinous, on their anniversary or at any time.

The incessant knocking at the door forced him to crawl from the bed and struggle into his clothes. "Just a minute," he yelled, wincing as he put a leg into his jeans.

Whoever was knocking banged as if they were trying to rip the door from its hinges.

"I said just a minute." More like five because every move was a reminder that his wife had felt the need to hurt him. So, unlike the beautiful, gentle woman he had married.

Terrence turned the knob, opening the door to find Roy Harper in mid-knock. The inn's owner wore a scowl that spoke of impatience.

"What is it?" Terrence demanded, taking in the red smoking jacket that was in clear contrast to the pasty man with thinning grey hair.

"What happened here, Mr. Reed?" Roy asked, trying to peer over Terrence's shoulder to take in the state of the room which held sure signs there had been a scuffle. The mattress was half off the bed, pillows strewn about the floor, and a vase of flowers had been turned over. Water ran over the edge of the writing desk and pooled on the Persian rug beneath.

"My wife and I were just … reacquainting ourselves with each other," Terrence answered angling to block the man's view. "Things got a little out of hand."

"Casey, it was an accident. Men miss the target sometimes." He'd never done it before this time, but they hadn't done it from that position, either.

A glance over his shoulder caused his gaze to land on the splotches of coppery liquid that stood out on the bright white sheets. The situation suddenly took a different slant. He'd been asking Casey to relax a little and try something different. A new position other than the missionary one they'd perfected. He'd been watching porn videos to get some ideas. She had tried a few other things, and he was anticipating a little bit of spice. Then he … well, what started out as spice, spiraled into an accident that somehow snowballed into her accusing him of rape.

His Pastor taught that wives were not supposed to deny their husbands anything. She had changed since the kids came along. It had been way too long since he was able to spend some quality time alone with Casey. She put everyone else on the front burner. The children. Her career. Her patients. Her parents. And he'd been patient and loving, hoping at some point he'd fit in her world. He thought this weekend would be a turning point for them. Where they could re-connect with each other and strengthen their bond.

Roy pushed past Terrence, entered the room and fixed a steely gaze on the blood stains. "Well, from what my wife told me, it got more than a little 'out of hand.' Why would you let her leave without clothes or shoes?" His gray-eyed gaze widened at the sight of the sheet.

"Maybe I should call the police." *The police.*

"As you can see," Terrence said, trying to keep the frustration from his voice. "I was just putting on my clothes to go after her when you interrupted. I can't go out there naked and barefoot."

"Why not? Your wife did," Roy challenged, his eyes locked disapprovingly on Terrence. "Must've been some dustup to cause a woman to be that afraid."

"You should mind your own business and stay out of mine," Terrence snapped.

His outburst caused Roy to lower his gaze. Terrence only had socks on his feet and wore a faded pair of jeans that he didn't dare zip up. "That's more than she left with. The hospital is one mile away. I figure it should take you all of thirty minutes walking. Less if you run."

"Do you have a car I could borrow?" Terrence inquired. "It'll be hard to get an Uber here."

Ray gave him a half-smile. "What happened to me minding my own business? Housekeeping will be up in ten minutes." With that, Roy's smile disappeared as he gave Terrence a warning glare, closed the door, and his hard footsteps echoed down the hallway.

Terrence tossed on a grey t-shirt and tried to fasten his jeans as he dialed a familiar number on his cell. A raspy older man answered, and Terrence confessed, "Gramps, I messed up."

"Boy, what you talkin' about?" Percy Reed said.

"Casey and I were having sex, and I slipped, and … um ..." Terrence replied, panicking. *What if Roy called the police? How would they see things?* "She's saying I raped her. Gramps, didn't you tell me there was no such thing as a wife being raped by her husband?"

"Boy hush now. You done slipped in the rooty tooty?" Gramps teased with a throaty chuckle.

Terrence was miffed that his grandfather could find humor in this situation. "She's at the hospital, she's … I hurt her … that's not —"

"I'm sure she enjoyed it. Even if she says she didn't, she did. That's how they all are. Don't have real brains. They're like children. We have to tell 'em how to think." Gramps spouted that antiquated logic through the phone. I'm kind a busy right now. Come by the house when you get back, and we'll talk. Go to the hospital so you can find out what she's saying to the doctors. I told you before, that one's no good. You're better off without her."

Terrence disconnected the call, unsettled by his grandfather's words. He never saw Casey as anything the old man described. She had a doctorate in psychology, a teaching license, academic awards, and she was the mother of his children. Now his wife was in the cold somewhere hurting, thinking he had intentionally harmed her. Already had the hotel owner's eyes accusing him of a crime.

"Casey, stop," Terrence shrieked, trying to get her to loosen her grip on his penis before he was never able to use it again. He shuddered with pain and tried to curl into himself, barely missing the blood spreading on the cotton sheets. Blood that was not his own.

"Oh my God, what have I done," he whispered.

Terrence watched Casey stumble into the bathroom. He should go after her, comfort her.

He was so excited that she had agreed to try a different position, doggy style, that he forgot he needed to be extra careful while back there. Hell, he thought she was enjoying it because her movements were so frantic. How was he supposed to know that she was screaming because she wanted him to stop? When he'd slipped up, he'd been so into it that he got caught up in the rush of feelings. By the time he'd realized something was wrong, the damage was already done. Now, Terrence needed his wife to understand this was an accident, and more importantly, that he hadn't violated her on purpose.

"Casey," Terrence cried as he banged on the wooden door that separated them. "Open the door," he implored her. "Please let me know you're alright." Again, he pounded on the door. "Casey please, I know you hear me."

"I'm sure everyone on this entire floor hears you," she snapped. "Unless you want company, I'd advise you to stop."

Willing the pain in his groin to go away Terrence leaned against the door. He waited a few minutes, thinking that she simply needed time to calm down.

"We can't hold a conversation through a door," Terrence said, as he knocked again.

"I need to go to the emergency room," Casey cried out.

Emergency room? Oh no! "Just come out of the bathroom, and I'll take you," Terrence pleaded, knowing it might take a minute before he was able to do anything, let alone get down the stairs.

"Step away from the door," Casey demanded.

Terrence complied, his bare feet shuffling against the bamboo wood floor. "You can come out now."

"If you lay a hand on me, I swear I'll scream until everyone in this place comes running."

She was afraid of him, and he didn't like it one bit.

"I promise not to touch you," he said in a low tone that he thought would soothe her. "Casey, I swear it was an accident."

The light tapping on the door pulled him from the memory and had him straightening the shirt on his body.

"Housekeeping," a soft voice said from the hallway.

"Coming," he replied, before making his way to the door.

"Give me a second, and I'll be out of your hair." The blonde middle-aged woman gave the room a quick scan but focused more on the bed. "Is that blood?" She frowned and yanked on a pair of plastic gloves as she waited for his response.

"Yes," he replied, grimacing at the reminder of exactly how hurt his wife had been.

"Where did it come from?" She swept a look over him. "You're not injured, are you?"

"My wife … started her monthly cycle," he answered. "She wasn't prepared, so she went to the drug store," he lied.

She lifted an eyebrow, then searched the room, spotting the clothing beneath a chair by the bathroom. She chanced another look at the bed, then to him, frowning again. Suspicion clouded her eyes. The lie had sounded weak to his own ears. Every woman kept track of things like that.

Terrence tied his shoe laces, and grabbed his wallet, jacket, phone, shoes, and some clothes for Casey before leaving the woman to clean up the mess.

When he made it to the bottom of the stairs, an undertaking that took a little time, a whole new ache hit him in the groin. He placed another call to his wife. No answer. Three more times, and each one went to voicemail. He couldn't walk to the end of the driveway, let alone an entire mile. Terrence called a cab.

He marveled at the intricate craftsmanship in the railings as he stood by the door waiting. Casey had made an excellent choice in this place that catered to the elite. In the past twelve hours, they'd been the only melanin-infused faces to grace the doorstep. From the looks of the place, he figured they hadn't had people of color other than waiting tables and cleaning.

The blaring horn caught his attention, and he grabbed Casey's bag, ignored the strange looks from Mr. Harper and entered the cab a few minutes later. Terrence tried to call again while en route, but it still rolled to voicemail.

He walked into the emergency room fifteen minutes later, bypassing an elderly gentleman standing at the front desk. "I'm trying to locate my wife, Casey Reed," he stated without giving either of the two nurses behind the desk time to ask how they could help.

"One second, sir, let me see if I can find her for you," the older nurse said.

A few pecks on the computer, and she locked her sky-blue eyes with Terrence's dark brown ones. "Let me find out if she can have visitors. Have a seat, please."

Terrence took a seat close to the window, so he wouldn't miss her return. His gaze landed on every person nearby, then to the magazines and pamphlets on the tables. Only then did he notice the elderly gentleman standing at the counter frowning. "Sir, I'm sorry I jumped in front of you," Terrence said. "I'm really worried about my wife."

"It's okay son. Thanks for the apology."

The nurse returned with a guy in a white coat and Terrence assumed he was the doctor until the man turned and walked away. The nurse motioned for Terrence to return to the window. "Dr. O'Malley will be right out to speak with you."

"Thank you, and I apologize for not waiting my turn like everyone else," Terrence said, an uneasy feeling creeping up his spine.

"You're welcome, sir," the nurse replied with a twenty-watt smile.

The doctor who had spoken with the nurse earlier came back into the waiting room with two other men flanking his side.

This can't be good.

"Mr. Reed, can I see your ID please?" the doctor asked, extending his hand to Terrence.

Sifting through his wallet, he handed over his license. "Can you tell me what's going on with my wife?"

"I'm Dr. O'Malley, and I'll be handling your wife's care. If you'd like to follow me, we can speak privately."

Terrence's gaze shot to the two men, waiting for an introduction that didn't come. He followed all three into a small conference room and the bulkiest of the three men shut the door behind him.

"Mrs. Reed suffered some injuries we're working to repair now. You wouldn't happen to know how they came about?" Dr. O'Malley asked.

One of the other men pulled out a pen and notepad awaiting Terrence's response.

"Doc, it was merely an accident," he said slowly. "I haven't been with my wife in a while. I got in the groove, and … I slipped. That's all that happened," Terrence explained.

"Her injuries are more consistent with ones we see in rape cases." *Rape. That word again.*

"Our nurse is getting some information at the moment. Detective Jacobson and Detective Winship have questions for you."

Terrence was well aware of how the police could take a small issue and make it five to ten. "I don't want to answer questions," Terrence retorted, stepping clear of the door. "I just want to see my wife."

"We can't allow you to see her while we're collecting evidence," Detective Winship stated.

Evidence.

"Can you tell me how much longer she'll be here?" Terrence asked, swallowing the knot that had formed in his throat.

Dr. O'Malley glanced at his watch. "Maybe another two to three hours, tops." As he stepped away, he added, "I must return to my patients."

One of the detectives moved forward, and his stance reminded Terrance of the ones who came at him after an unfortunate incident in college.

"I'm not answering any questions without a lawyer present." Terrence thrust Casey's bag toward the detectives. "Please give these to my wife." That said, he walked out the door.

Rape. Evidence. Questions.

Somehow Terrence got the feeling that his mistake was going to cost him more than he imagined.

Chapter 4

The snow outside of Cedar Crest Inn should have melted from the heat flowing off Terrence. Hot was an understatement for his condition. The nerve of those detectives, acting like he was a common criminal. He had made a mistake. Since when was that a crime?

He called the one person he knew had a response for every problem. Terrence wished it was his dad, but that tie had been severed a long time ago when he walked out of his parent's house at seventeen.

"Gramps," he said as soon as his grandfather wheezed into the phone.

"Boy, what you want now? I told you to call when you got back." Percy protested, as if Terrence was interrupting something.

He stepped on the wrap-around porch, out of earshot of other guests in the lobby before he continued. "I know, but I went to the hospital and detectives were already there wanting to question me. I need a lawyer."

"What?" his grandfather exclaimed. "This is ridiculous, but don't worry, I'll have someone on standby when you get home."

"Thanks, Gramps, I love you, man," Terrence said, sighing with relief. "Yeah, yeah, I love you, boy," Percy replied.

Terrence went inside and took a seat at a table near the window overlooking the snow-covered patio. He perused the Inn's menu for a few minutes before making a breakfast choice. He tried to call Casey one more time. When the voicemail kicked in, he said, "Casey, please call me when you get this message. I just … I need to know you're okay." As he shoved the cell into his pocket, it brushed against his bruised genitals, and he winced.

A red-haired, spry-for-her-age waitress appeared at the table. "Good morning, my name is Lilly. Have you decided what you want?"

"I'll have a cup of coffee, two eggs over easy, some grits, bacon, and two slices of toast."

She jotted that on her notepad, "I'll get your order in," and gestured to a spot behind her. "Beverages are right over there."

"Thanks."

As he made his way to the self-service bar, he inhaled the wonderful aroma of fresh baked bread and breakfast meats and fixed a cup of black coffee. Returning to his table to wait for breakfast, he replayed what happened in the early morning hours. He grew even more convinced that Casey's behavior was pure drama. She had to know that he'd never intentionally hurt her. She was his wife, after all. He would get her to understand that when he saw her again. A small voice inside whispered, *if you see her again.*

Panic flared for a moment but dissipated. Terrence ran a hand over his stubbled jaw, the strain of the last few hours evident in the anxiety coursing through his mind. Of course, she'd come back to him. He wasn't a monster out to defile his wife. The sooner she understood that, the sooner they could put this simple misunderstanding behind them.

Within ten minutes, Lilly arrived with his breakfast in hand. Everything looked delectable, and despite everything, he had a mammoth appetite.

"I hope you enjoy," she said warmly. "Please let me know if you need anything else."

"Thank you for the excellent service," Terrence said, giving her a warm smile.

He enjoyed his food and though satisfied physically, he missed his wife and wanted her back with him. This was supposed to be their weekend getaway.

Finishing his meal, he returned to their freshly-cleaned suite to wait with only memories, candles, and a reality television show to keep him company.

An hour later, Casey still hadn't called. What could be keeping her? Maybe what the doctor said was far worse than he thought. Probably some emotional issues. Gramps always said women were a little dense. Casey was many things, but dense she wasn't. However, he'd never forget the look she'd given him just before she rushed from the room. Her face was twisted in disgust. Maybe even hatred.

"No," he said aloud. "She could never hate me. We're married, we have kids. She might be pissed off now, but eventually she'll come around."

Feeling better, Terrence busied himself with making sure everything in the room was ready for when she returned. Fresh linens were already in place, as well as a new floral arrangement. The vanilla candles infused the air with a pleasant aroma. The setting was back to being romantic. Just like it had been the night before. They'd do it right this time. He would definitely avoid any experimental things. Just missionary for a while.

He didn't want to rock the boat or upset Casey. Then again, the man was the head of the wife. He reached for the Bible on the desk and turned to the scripture that said wives should submit to their husbands in everything. As he read the words, his resolve grew. He was the head of his household. He would make Casey see that his actions weren't calculated. That he'd just gotten caught up in the moment and overwhelmed by the sensations. He'd never do so again without her permission, but she needed to forgive him. To get past last night's trauma so they could move on. She had to forgive him.

The Bible said so.

Chapter 5

Olivia Whitaker eased the comforter into a plastic evidence bag, then scraped under Casey's nails for DNA. She also took pictures, paying attention to the bruising and tearing. After the exam, Olivia provided hospital scrubs for Casey to wear after her shower.

Casey raised her head to the soft knocks at the door. "Yes, who's there?"

"Ms. Reed, it's Olivia. I have a bag of clothes your husband dropped off, if you would like to put those on instead." "Come in," Casey whispered.

Olivia entered the room, carrying Casey's chevron overnight bag.

"He came here?" she asked. Her trembling hand flew to her mouth.

"The detectives said he refused to answer their questions." Olivia bit her lip before adding, "He said what happened to you was a misunderstanding and genuinely seemed concerned for your wellbeing."

"If he'd really been concerned for my well-being I wouldn't be here," Casey snapped. "I'd still be in our suite celebrating our anniversary, wouldn't I?"

"Only you know the answer to that question," Olivia stated before turning and leaving the room.

Casey finished dressing, gathered her belongings, and exited the hospital with more dignity than she felt when she'd arrived. Her first stop was the pharmacy to fill prescriptions for painkillers and an antibiotic. The doctor had advised that the medication she was given at the hospital should keep her comfortable until she got home. Her main concern was getting back to the inn to pack up the rest of her things. She wanted to go home and find comfort in her own bed. She had already called her office to reschedule her more critical clients for the next week. Another therapist would take over for her as long as she needed. Based on her injuries, sitting for long periods of time at work wasn't something she'd be able to handle.

Five stitches, internally.

Casey slid through the door of the inn and came face to face with Mrs. Harper. She felt a bit self-conscious after the state that the woman had seen her in last night. Casey was so out of it that she hadn't even remembered saying goodbye to her at the hospital.

"Mrs. Harper, thank you so much for all you did for me last night. I'm sorry I didn't get a chance to thank you before you left the hospital."

The woman's eyes glazed over with tears of sympathy, as she replied, "Please, call me Margaret, dear. No apology is necessary, Dr. Reed. I was happy to help you in any way I could."

Warmth spread from her heart all the way down to her feet at the concern etched in Margaret's face and her words. "Thank you."

At a loss for what else to say, Casey hung her head as she headed toward the stairs. The magnitude of the situation lay heavily on her shoulders.

A small, weathered hand touched her shoulder. It was enough to make her pause. Startled, Casey turned around.

"Dr. Reed, please hold your head up. You have nothing to be ashamed of," Margaret whispered. "None of these people know anything about your situation, except me and my husband Roy. The maid that was sent to clean the room just believes you started your cycle, based on what your husband said. Her job depends on being discreet, so she'll never say a word, I promise."

Casey mouthed the words, "Thank you" and continued up the stairs, but this time with her head held high.

* * *

In her room, Casey grabbed her things and crushed them into a suitcase stretched out on the bed. She walked to the nightstand and removed her cellphone and turned it on.

Terrence, who'd been sitting in the room awaiting her return, looked on from his spot near a desk sitting by the window.

"I wish you'd talk to me," he said getting to his feet. "That's why you didn't get my calls. What'd the doctor say?"

She didn't reply. Instead, she focused her efforts on placing the rest of her things in the overnight bag and putting as much distance between herself, this place, and him, as possible.

Grabbing her hand to still her movements, he asked, "Can you stop for one minute and talk to me?"

She snatched her hand away. Casey hesitated for a moment, wanting to ignore him altogether. "We have to check out in thirty minutes. I insisted on paying for the incidentals even though the owners didn't ask." She lifted a lacy negligee and tossed it in with the rest of her new purchases. "According to the physician, I'll be fine once I heal. The police wanted to know who did this to me, but you already know that since you were at the hospital."

Terrence opened his mouth to protest, but she held up a hand to ward him off.

"I just want to go home, hug my kids, and forget this happened." Terrence reached for her, but she stepped aside, bypassing him to hurry into the bathroom to gather up the toiletries spread out on the counter. A single teardrop escaped from her eye. She wiped it away with the back of her hand and willed the rest of the tears to stay put. Not once had the words, "I'm sorry" passed his lips. She refused to break down in front of him.

He grabbed his gym bag and tossed his clothing and toiletries in without even a second glance to see if he missed anything. "I did go to the hospital because I needed to check up on you. I was worried."

Casey zipped her bags shut and said, "Were you? Or did you just want to make sure I didn't drop your name to the cops?" Casey walked toward the door, as he rushed forward to keep up with her.

"I don't care about that. It was an accident, and nothing more. You know I'd never intentionally hurt you," Terrence insisted.

Continuing her path down the stairs to the lobby, she threw over her shoulder "The police talked with the nurse. It's hospital protocol to report the kind of injuries that I sustained."

"What did you say when they talked to you?" Terrence asked. He'd been worried about the police involvement and needed to understand the implications of his actions. When he spotted the bed and breakfast owners, his questions ceased.

Margaret pulled Casey to the side, "Although I'm not privy to everything that happened, I could guess from that look of fear in your eyes that it was very traumatic. If you need help, please let me know." As she spoke, she slipped two cards into Casey's hand and curled her own around both. "The first card is mine, and the second belongs to an attorney friend of mine who'll be awaiting your call, should you feel the need. Also, I refunded the deposit for the incidentals to your account. Consider it my gift to you."

"Mr. Reed, a word please," Roy said. He tried to steer him away from Margaret and Casey, but Terrence stood firm.

"Yes sir, what can I do for you?" Terrence sighed, impatience in his tone.

"Take better care of your wife, or someone else may do it for you." Terrence's face contorted with anger. "I'll take care of mine. If you want to help with something, help with the bags."

This request was met with blank stares from the owners, who then turned and walked away.

***

"Let's go, Casey," Terrence growled.

Casey eased into the passenger side on the doughnut the pharmacy had suggested she purchase. Terrence kept his eyes on her every inch of the way while she maneuvered into the seat, and she refused to let it unsettle her.

He slid behind the wheel and grabbed her hand saying, "You still didn't tell me what you said, baby."

Casey instantly extracted her hand from his. She pulled away from him and folded her hands in her lap before saying, "I told them the truth."

"What's that supposed to mean?"

"I told them every minute detail of what happened in the room, and that my husband raped me."

"Why would you tell them that? I told you it was an accident. I just slipped," Terrence said as he maneuvered the car on to the two-lane road.

Casey took in the passing scenery, which included the Blue Ridge Mountains. Even though she had seen them on several occasions, this time the view of the mountains put her in a more serene state.

"Why'd you say that to the police?" Terrence asked again as he tapped his fingers on the armrest. "I admit, I got caught up in the moment. I was just overcome. It never should've happened."

"You're telling me?" she shot back. "I was not going to lie. Why are you so worried about what I said? It was all in fun, right?"

"You know better than that. It started out that way, but—" Terrence stopped for a moment to compose himself. He was gripping the steering wheel a little too tightly. "That wasn't … it wasn't rape. I … I …."

"I don't want to talk about it anymore," Casey said, dismissively. She switched the satellite radio from the hip-hop he preferred to a station where the smooth jazz sounds of Kim Waters serenaded her. She relaxed a little as the music flowed through the speakers and flooded the car with a melodious interlude.

They'd only driven an hour, with the music as a distraction and a balm when Terrence stopped at a rest area in Haywood County to use the restroom and stretch. Casey waited until Terrence was out of range, pulled out her phone and dialed a number she dreaded.

"Hey, baby," came her mother's southern drawl. Her mother had grown up in North Carolina.

"Mom, we're on our way home," Casey said as she watched the activities around her. A young couple with their chunky toddler, a bald gentleman checking the cargo perched on top of his truck, and a stunning lady with silver hair walking her dog.

"That's early isn't it? I wasn't expecting you for another day."

Casey wasn't in the mood for drawn-out conversations about this trip. The longer she talked to her mother, the easier it would be for her to pick up on her mood. No way was she ready for the third degree. "Can you just have Skye and TJ ready in an hour and thirty minutes?"

"Drive safely. We'll talk when you get here." She disconnected the call before Casey could get in another word.

Terrence stood in the distance several feet away by the vending machines, talking on his phone. He flailed both arms in full hysterics as he spoke into his Bluetooth.

She wondered what warranted such a dramatic conversation, then frowned. It could only be Percy Reed on the other end of the line. He could definitely get under your skin quickly. That old man had never liked Casey and the feeling was mutual.

Terrence ended his call and stormed toward the car, heavy steps eating up the pavement.

Reclaiming his seat, he closed his eyes and took a few deep breaths. When he finally turned to her, he was calm. "I was hoping we could go home first, spend some time alone before we picked up the kids." Everything inside Casey screamed.

"You can't be serious right now?" she said through her teeth. "We just spent the entire weekend together and look how that turned out."

"Casey—"

"I'm sure you know that's not going to happen," she snapped. "I need time."

His mouth opened.

"And don't even bother to ask how much," she said before he could speak.

Terrence's jaw clenched as he flexed his hand, as though he wanted to punch something.

"My mother will have Skye and TJ ready when we arrive." The rest of the drive was made in silence.

Chapter 6

Phillip and Ella Henderson lived in a single-family brick home in Charlotte, North Carolina. The community was known for well-kept lawns, close-knit families, and little kids running through the safe neighborhood. Casey had grown up with strict parents, loyal friends, and her beloved dog, Smokey. Backyard barbecues, stolen kisses, the first crush, first loves, and the dreaded fall from the first ride on a bike. All the love that a married couple could bestow on a child, her parents had managed to give.

After dating through junior high, her parents had become lovers in high school. By the time they graduated, Casey was on the way. They eloped against their parent's wishes and though struggling at the beginning, they stuck it out despite all the naysayers. Overcoming challenge after challenge had made their marriage stronger but seemed to have an adverse effect on Casey's. Their marriage had been turbulent for the first year due to Percy's interference, but became conventional afterwards. She guessed it was the calm before the storm because now all hell was about to break loose.

Easing out of the car, Casey walked gingerly up the path and entered her parent's elegantly furnished home. When she spotted her kids, she wrapped them up in her arms. Skye was a rambunctious little girl whose features were a blend of her and Terrence. Their daughter inherited Casey's dark hair but had natural curls and hazel eyes. She had Terrance's nose and inherited his stubbornness. TJ was a perfect likeness of his father. with his thick eyebrows, caramel complexion, long lean fingers, strong legs, and dark brown eyes that seemed to stare straight through a person.

"Hi, babies," Casey said as she tried to bend over to pick up TJ and realized she couldn't. The pain pills may have kicked in, but certain movements brought a stark reminder that she was not alright. She kissed his face before giving Skye one on her forehead.

"How's my big girl?"

"Mommy look what I painted for you and Daddy," she beamed, handing over a piece of colored construction paper with a crude drawing.

"This is beautiful, Skye," Casey said, taking the opportunity to encourage her child even though she wasn't sure what the picture represented. It could've been a giraffe or a flower, who knew?

"I made it for you and Daddy," she said. "A present for your anniversary."

Anniversary. Mrs. Reed, you're going to need stitches.

"Well thank you, my sweetheart, I appreciate it," Casey said pushing the ugly thoughts aside. "Now grab your things so we can go, please."

Casey, who had momentarily lost her manners, glanced at her mom and said, "Hi Mom, how are you?" She took in her mother's observant gaze and inhaled, bracing herself for the questions that were certain to come. She never walked into her parents' home without speaking to them first.

Ella was a beautiful, gracious woman with mahogany skin as smooth as whipped butter that was proof that women of color aged gracefully. Casey knew her mom was waiting for her to acknowledge she was in the room. She decided against her normal routine of twirling TJ around and then giving a whirl to Skye. Her daughter was getting a little heavier, so her turn usually didn't last long.

"I'm fine, but a better question is, how are you?" Her mother asked without taking her eyes off Casey.

She sidestepped the small woman and tried to straighten her movements to seem normal as she aimed for the two little bags near the door. "Everything's good. I've got to go. Terrence is in the car."

"Well, he could've got out of it to help get the kids to the car," she said in a dry tone. "In fact, the way you're walking, it looks as if he should've been the one to handle the entire process."

Casey winced as her mom's words cut deep. She never had anything bad to say about Terrence. To her, since he had a job, paid the mortgage, and took care of his children, he practically walked on water.

"We're fine. I'll call you later," she yelled back as she ushered the kids down the pathway and tried, truly tried, to make it look like the slow steps had everything to do with balancing the bags.

"Casey, wait," Ella said with concern. "Since you obviously aren't feeling well, just leave the kids. I'll bring them home tomorrow."

Casey had already made the short distance to the car and wanted to take her mother up on her offer but making the trip back up that path would give too much away.

Opening the door to strap TJ in, Terrence asked, "What's up with you? Why are you so distressed?"

"Mom just asked that I leave the kids, since I wasn't feeling well," Casey said in a matter of fact tone.

Terrence glanced at the house where his mother-in-law was watching from the porch. "Did you tell her anything?"

"No, now can you stop asking what I'm telling people?" Casey snapped. She secured TJ and slid into the passenger seat, waving at her mother, whose expression remained the same.

"Mommy show Daddy the picture I painted," Skye crooned.

Casey held out the drawing. "Here."

He glanced at the picture briefly. "This is cute, baby girl. I'll have to buy a frame for it."

Content that her dad loved her artwork, Skye pulled out a book from the bag on the seat next to hers. TJ played with the toys attached to his car seat. Neither child was interested in the grown-up activity in the front seat.

"Why don't we let them stay and you can get some rest. I'll pick them up tomorrow," Terrence suggested.

Casey felt a surge of relief. "Fine, but you walk them back to my mom," she huffed.

Terrence gathered the kids and their bags but before he closed the door she said, "I'd love to hear what you're going to tell her when she asks what's wrong with me." *Five stitches, Terrence.*

Five.

Chapter 7

The vibration in the pocket of her blazer stopped District Attorney Adah Osmani on her path to the courtroom. "Hello."

"Adah, this is Margaret Harper," came the hushed voice on the other end. "Do you have a moment?"

Adah pushed the designer shades to the top of her head to hold back the dark hair that flowed down her back, then placed an Italian leather briefcase on the bench. "I have about an hour before giving my closing argument for a trial that's been going on for the last two years. I take it this is a business call?"

"You would be correct in that assumption," she replied. "There's a couple that was here over the weekend. I believe the wife was raped."

Adah was silent for a spell as the flow of foot traffic from bailiffs, attorneys, and anxious family members swelled around her.

"Did you witness the assault?" Adah asked, taking a seat next to her briefcase.

"No, but something bad happened for this woman to run from her room without a stitch of clothing, wrapped in a bloody blanket, and nothing on her feet. She was in such a bad way I had to drive her to the hospital."

Adah absorbed this information, checked her watch and remembered Mrs. Harper, a former director at the Rape Crisis Center, would know all the signs. She also had called in very few favors over the years, so this one had to be important.

"Alright. Do me a favor and give her my info and tell her to call me."

"I slipped her your card before she left. She's a Black woman. Didn't seem to want to open up to me, probably because I'm White."

"Having a different ethnic background shouldn't make a difference. She's a woman who needs help regardless of her color. Besides, it didn't stop you from helping me, a woman of Pakistani descent," Adah replied to her friend. "Or maybe it's because most women don't run around spreading their business to strangers."

"Roy said the husband was defensive and tight-lipped."

"Based on experience, men tend to be that way if they're on the wrong end of a possible eight to twenty-year bid. I'll check with the detectives and see if they were called by the hospital. Looks like I'll be finishing this trial just in time. Mrs. Harper, thank you for continuing to care about women's welfare," Adah replied to her friend.

"Now Adah, you know there's nothing that gives me greater joy than helping a woman escape a bad situation. Thanks for taking the call. Best of luck on the trial."

Adah placed her phone back in her briefcase and scanned the sour faces of the accuser's and the defendant's family members. She was so ready for this trial to be over. They had exhausted every witness and the defense had fought hard to keep from convicting this man. Adah had been surprised that her ex-husband hadn't been given this case since it was high profile. Khalid loved the spotlight. Instead the defendant was stuck with Greg Wallace, a court-appointed attorney. Months of back and forth had almost worn her client into backing out.

Especially with the media frenzy surrounding the defendant, the owner of Green's Mortuary. Adah walked into the courtroom, nodding at the defense attorney before engaging the assistant district attorney.

Court began as normal with the bailiff doing his routine of calling the court to order before the judge addressed counsel and the jury. Adah couldn't wait to give her closing argument. As far as she was concerned this had been an open and shut case. Only the defense bringing in multiple character witnesses and experts had made it drag on forever.

Adah faced the jury to give her closing statement and said, "Ladies and gentlemen of the jury. You've heard and seen the evidence that has been played out before you over the last several months." She paced the floor in front of the jury box and pointed across the courtroom. "The defense will have you believe that their client, Mr. Green, is a great father and husband ..." Thoughts and images of her ex-spouse clouded her mind, she quickly refocused. "He's a hard worker and good provider for his family. A deacon in the church, and a faithful tither."

Again, all outward qualities that made her thoughts wander to her ex-husband and how his culture's archaic beliefs affected their marriage. Khalid, and the bulk of his male family members, believed that women should be submissive and had no say in a marriage. Despite the fact that some women earned more than their male counterparts, Adah believed that marriage was a partnership. Somehow, they were on opposite sides of the marriage spectrum. Understanding that from the start would've saved ten years, two children, a mortgage, joint finances and a whole lot of grief on her part.

"While all these things may be true, it doesn't negate the fact that Mr. Green is a meticulous cold-hearted rapist." She paused to look at the defendant and let that sink in. "We proved beyond a shadow of a doubt that the defendant deliberately and consistently kept his wife in a drug-induced stupor. This alone is incriminating enough because the defendant provided the evidence himself." Adah stopped to let this resonate with the jury. She took her seat next to a stocky man in a crisp designer suit and waited as the defense began his closing remarks.

Mr. Wallace, an attorney with a medium build, bald head, unibrow, red face, wearing a gray jacket over a sweater and black pants addressed the jury. "The prosecution has failed to shape a case that would make anyone with common sense believe this was rape. Mr. Green was under extreme duress and desired the comfort of his wife. Is that so wrong?" Wallace looked at Mrs. Green and smirked as he recounted some of the facts he had laid out during the course of the trial, ending with, "Ladies and gentlemen of the jury, he may have videotaped an intimate act between him and his spouse, but that's not against the law. Surely some of you have had less than "normal" sexual fantasies between you and your partner and wanted to capture that moment for later enjoyment. Mr. Green was simply exploring his fantasies with the woman he loves. That is not a crime." Wallace assessed the expectant faces of the jurors. "You have no choice but to acquit my client of all the charges against him."

The noise from the unruly onlookers and the angered members of the victim's family drowned out the wooden mallet striking the sound block.

"Order in the court," the judge said banging the gavel. "I'll have order in this court room."

The family of the victim had every reason to be irate that Wallace was trying to get Mr. Green off.

"I'll kill him myself," shouted someone on the victim's family's side of the court room.

"Give me five minutes alone with him," shouted another.

The threats being yelled had everyone snapping their heads to see who was speaking, especially the bailiff. Two burly guys, who looked more like nightclub bouncers, stood at the back door while two smaller guys guarded each door in the front of the court room which led to the judge's chambers. The judge had requested tighter security after a death threat came into his office and Adah's office, promising that things would not turn out well for them if the defendant got off.

Again, the judge yelled, "I'll have order in this court, or the bailiff will escort everyone out."

Murmurs of dissent filled the packed courtroom, but the outrage settled to a mere whisper. Adah Osmani faced the jury again to counter the defense's closing statement.

"The defense has tried to convince you that the defendant did nothing wrong. The problem with the video is that if the complainant was unconscious, how did she consent to the act? While she was in a drug induced state, he took videos of himself being intimate with her. She did not participate. She couldn't. You saw them. She was lifeless. Why? Because she was drugged. He took away her voice. He ensured she could not say "no," or "stop," Adah stated. "He did things to her which he knew she would not approve. Then he had the utter gall to record it, so he could relive her degradation at his leisure." Adah paced in front of the jurors then moved toward the defendant. "Yes, she's his wife, but she's also a woman who deserves his consideration and respect. He raped her as if she were nothing. This God-fearing, honored deacon, and faithful tither forgot that even his own Bible says love thy neighbor as you would yourself. Could you condone this happening to you?"

The jurors—mostly men— shifted in their seats. Adah's gaze bounced from each man on the jury. She wanted them thinking and focused for her next statement. She pointed a finger at each one as she said, "Juror number one, your daughter? Juror number five, your niece, and juror number eight, your sisters? How about you, juror number two, your … mother?"

"My God," juror number two uttered.

"If you can't see it happening to them, what makes it right for it to happen to Mrs. Green? Isn't she a woman, too?" Adah paused to let this sink into the crevices of their minds. "All because she bears the title of wife? All because he has a sheet of paper that signifies marriage? When did that mean she doesn't matter? For this reason, you must find him guilty as charged."

One of the jurors, a silver haired woman, chanced a look at Mr. Green.

"Your Honor, the prosecution rests." Adah reclaimed her seat and glanced at Mrs. Green, who was crying on the row behind her.

After instructing the jury to solely judge on the facts and credibility of witnesses, and to base their conclusions only on the evidence as presented in the trial, the judge recessed the courtroom while they deliberated.

* * *

"So now we wait," Wallace said, as he stepped into the hallway where Adah stood checking her messages. She stared at his gray goatee, which still had breadcrumbs lodged in it as if he was storing them for a later meal.

"How did you end up with this case?" Adah asked something that she had wondered from day one. His appearance matched his disjointed handling of the case. One would think this was his first case, though she knew he'd been a district attorney at one time. Wallace noticed her staring and adjusted his clothes.

"I was his court-appointed attorney," he answered. "Since my divorce, I've taken on some of the defense attorney's cases so I could get my foot back in the door. I still have to pay my alimony."

"You don't have to explain your history to me," she said, but inwardly she was glad he mentioned all of it. "However, I do have a question. Why are you defending this creep?" She asked.

"No one ever said I had to believe him. They only pay me to defend him." His expression appeared defeated. "At one time, I would've been the one to string men like Mr. Green up," he whispered.

At that moment both of their cell phones vibrated. The jury was back in after deliberating for only two hours. Each lawyer spared a quick glance at each other before grabbing their belongings and entering the courtroom. As they walked down the marble tiled hallway toward the courtroom, Adah rehearsed the words Wallace said, "They only pay me to defend him." She knew there was more to this, but she would worry about Wallace later. Her thoughts now turned to her failed marriage, one that had similar issues as Mrs. Green, but not to the point where her husband had drugged her. No, Khalid's actions were emotional and physical abuse. Time healed the bruises and physical injuries, while the Buncombe County Rape Crisis Center had done a lot to repair her fractured spirit. The center had empowered her and gave her the voice she never had.

Now cases like these were her life. She won a good majority of them, mostly because juries despised men who violated women. Sometimes the laws didn't allow for open and shut cases. The woman Mrs. Harper called about could be one of those cases. Marital rape laws differed from state to state. As soon as this case was over, Adah planned to investigate more about what had transpired at Cedar Crest Inn.

"All rise," the bailiff said, as the judge entered the court room.

"Has the jury reached a verdict, Mr. Foreman?" the judge asked a few moments after he was seated.

A thirty-something year-old Black male stood, his expression giving away nothing as he replied. "Yes, Your Honor, we have."

"The defendant will please stand," the judge said, causing Wallace and, Mr. Green to rise.

"In the case of The State of North Carolina vs. Green, how do you find?" the judge asked.

Adah reached over the banister and held Mrs. Green's hand and offered her a reassuring smile.

"We the jury find the defendant guilty of rape in the second degree."

The court erupted with celebratory cheers as the verdict came down. Mr. Green's mother sat crying in a handkerchief, while Mrs. Green hugged Adah, saying, "Thank you for everything." Then she walked over to comfort her mother-in-law, who had been the lone supporter for her son.

Adah accepted the woman's gratitude with humility, but her mind was already whirling with thoughts about the woman who held her card.

Chapter 8

Terrence escorted the children back to his mother-in-law, then he and Casey were on their way home to the two-story brick colonial nestled in St. Andrews, South Carolina. They chose to settle there because Casey did not want to live more than an hour from her mother. Within twenty minutes, Casey was medicated and working in the kitchen, steam was rising from pots, and the house smelled like home. She turned to find Terrence standing behind her. She stepped around him and returned to the stove.

"Are you okay?"

"Just fine," she replied, focusing on the final touches for dinner.

He nodded. "I'm going to wash the car."

Casey didn't respond. When dinner was ready, she fixed her plate and sat down to eat. When Terrence reentered the kitchen some time later, he scanned the table and frowned.

"Where's my plate?"

"The food is on the stove, and the plates are where they normally are. Feel free to help yourself," she answered without taking her focus off of loading the dishwasher.

Terrence stomped past her, mumbling under his breath.

After washing his hands, Terrence turned toward his wife. "Can we talk, Casey?"

"What is it?"

"You can't fix my plate anymore? When we got married, you said that you'd loved waiting on me."

"Excuse me if I don't feel like I need to respect a man that disrespected me," Casey said as she exited the kitchen.

Casey walked upstairs to their bedroom. Closing the door firmly behind her, she kicked off her shoes and padded to the bathroom. Once there, she prepared a warm Epsom salt bath, then she gently eased into the hot water and soaked her throbbing, achy body.

An hour later, Casey was wide awake. Even though she was dead tired, sleep didn't come easy. Her mind was racing about what would happen when her husband came to bed. She didn't have long to wait. A few minutes later, Terrence slid in beside her and every movement he made was exaggerated. The king size bed seemed so much smaller than its actual size.

Neither of them said goodnight. Instead, both turned on their sides away from each other.

Terrence slept peacefully, snoring in his normal range while she beat her pillow trying to get comfortable. How could he just walk in the room and be asleep in less than five minutes? Terrence rolled and dropped his arm over Casey's side. She froze; her skin crawled from his touch. "Get your hands off me," she shrieked, and scrambled off the bed.

Terrence sat up in bed. "What's wrong with you?" He struggled to turn on the lamp.

He left the bed and placed his hand on her shoulder, trying to calm her down. "I'm not going to hurt you," he pleaded. "Please look at me."

She recoiled from even the slightest touch. Stepping out of his reach to stand beside the chair, she steadied her breathing, focusing on the patterns in the carpet as she counted out loud.

"I think you need to see someone," he said, concerned. "Gramps was right. Women are seriously mental."

Her head whipped toward him, and anger somehow took a front seat to her fear. "What would Percy know? He hasn't been in a serious relationship since your grandmother left him thirty years ago. You have the audacity to tell me that I need help. Don't you understand what you've done?" Regaining her composure, she grabbed her robe from the chair and left the room.

Terrence followed her down the hallway, asking, "Wait, where are you going?"

"I can't stand you touching me right now," she said through clenched teeth. "I was hoping you'd have the common sense to sleep in the guest room. Just go back to sleep and keep pretending nothing happened."

"I'm not pretending nothing happened. I'm merely trying to help us move past it. How long are you going to punish me? I told you I was sorry."

"They gave me five stitches, you clueless idiot. That doesn't sound like a mistake to me. It sounds more like you wanted control. You can't stand not being in control, and in your own sick way, you were trying to gain it back."

He blanched at those words. His face paled, and his cheeks reddened.

"That's not true."

"Isn't it?"

"I apologized," he countered, as she slowly backed out the door. "What more do you need from me?"

"When?" she shot back. "When did you apologize? Cause I certainly didn't hear a sincere apology come out of your mouth. I heard 'mistake' and 'something new.' She stepped back into his space. "I heard that you wanted to spend time alone. Seriously? On what planet was that supposed to happen?"

Casey poked him in the chest "I heard all of that, yet you never heard my plea."

Chapter 9

The following week, Terrence sat in his office at Columbia Automotive Group, working on sales budgets for the year. He was finding it hard to concentrate on his work with his marriage spiraling out of control. He'd forgotten to go over to his grandfather's house after they returned. His father had given him a stern warning about listening to the old man's outdated way of thinking. But he needed someone to discuss this with, and since Casey wanted counseling, he thought of the next best step and then called his Pastor.

Pastor Jim Faircloth, at the age of sixty-five, had been married twice before. Each wife had left under suspicious circumstances that no one from his church would discuss. The media ran a segment about it, but instead of inciting folks to leave, membership had increased. Now he was on wife number three.

"May I speak with Pastor Faircloth?"

"May I ask who's calling, please?" came a pleasant voice on the other side.

"This is Terrence Reed."

After a brief pause, she said "Hold, please. I'll transfer the call."

Pastor Faircloth picked up the line a few moments later. "Good morning, Brother Reed. How may I help you?"

"I'd like to schedule a few counseling sessions for me and my wife."

The Pastor coughed and then shuffled some papers on the other end. "I guess I can fit you in for a few. When would you like to start?"

"How about tonight or tomorrow?" Terrence asked, wanting to get this hiccup in the marriage under control as quickly as possible. He wanted his wife back.

"Tonight, will work fine. Just fine," Pastor coughed out. "See you tonight at six o'clock."

"See you then, Pastor," Terrence said, breathing a sigh of relief. "Thank you for seeing us on such short notice."

A few counseling sessions with the Reverend, and Casey would see things in a new light. She would see that he wasn't the bad guy. Even if he didn't mean to do it, didn't the Bible say 'Wives, submit yourselves unto your own husbands'? So why was she acting like he would purposefully cause her pain? He loved her and their family.

One reason he chose this church was because Pastor Faircloth leaned more to the Old Testament way of thinking. He was a stickler for women remaining silent in the church and the man having control over his household. If anyone dared to speak out against Pastor Faircloth's teachings, as Casey had on prior occasions, their spouses were quickly told to get them in line. While Terrence didn't agree with everything Pastor Faircloth taught, he'd admit he liked not having his decisions questioned or having to clear financial or household decisions with anyone. They had been members at the church for the last three years. Casey had been reluctant to attend because she didn't always agree with the Pastor. Ultimately, Terrence's persistence won out, and Casey finally joined. She had been having a hard time though, unlike the way it had been at the beginning of their marriage.

The next call he made was to Casey. None of this worked if she didn't agree to attend along with him. He anxiously paced the floor waiting on her to answer, and after the fifth ring, he almost thought she wouldn't. "What?" Casey said upon hearing his voice.

He flinched at her tone. "Hey, baby, I scheduled an appointment for us with Pastor Faircloth. It's at six o'clock tonight."

"Of course, you'd pick him," she snapped. "Shouldn't you have checked with me to make sure my schedule was free?"

Terrence tempered an angry retort as he gripped the edge of his desk. "Well, you wanted counseling, and I took the initiative. I thought you canceled your appointments for the week. Where are you anyway?"

"I'm sitting on the couch, going over case notes for the next week." Pecking on the keyboard echoed from her end. After a few minutes, she responded, "If I recall, you demanded I get counseling. I'd think you would've let me choose someone that I trust."

"I'm sorry," Terrence replied, deflated. "I was trying to help."

Casey expelled a deep breath. "Next time please call me before you schedule appointments that require my presence."

Terrence never had a chance to respond. She hung up without even saying goodbye.

* * *

The next few hours flew by as he worked on the projections. He believed would secure his promotion and increase profitability by eight percent. His job was on the line if he didn't. They had already lost several valuable members of the staff due to the company's morality clause, something he felt was a trap to get rid of employees, since revenue had decreased also.

Five o'clock rolled around fast. Terrence closed out his files and shut his computer down. Grabbing his briefcase, he strolled past the receptionist's desk and out the entrance. Thankfully she was away from her desk, and he wouldn't have to spend the next fifteen minutes listening to her try in vain to flirt with him.

Forty-five minutes later, Terrence parked in one of the available spaces closest to the church. Needing to provide a united front, he waited for Casey outside. Within five minutes, Casey was pulling her car in the parking lot with ten minutes to spare. He should've known she would be on time. She was punctual if nothing else. He relaxed a bit. Pastor

Faircloth would set things straight. Casey might not respect the man, but she did respect the Bible.

Terrence left his Jeep Cherokee and made a beeline through the empty spaces to her Lexus RX. He leaned in to kiss her faster than she was able to step out of the car.

Casey recoiled back into the car and said, "You're five seconds away from getting smacked. Now move. Five, four, three, two—"

Terrence hesitated, shocked by the tone that matched her scowl.

"Why are you so angry?" he asked as he moved away, keeping an eye on her while allowing her to move past him.

"Why are you out here acting like we have a perfect marriage and that you typically open the car door for me?" she snapped, glancing toward the second story window where Pastor Faircloth was watching. "Let him see the real man that you are, not the one that only does nice stuff for his wife when he feels his marriage is threatened." Terrence walked at her side in silence.

The two entered the plush sanctuary, which catered to the tastes of the five hundred middle class to wealthy members. The church was home to lawyers, doctors, professional athletes, and politicians. The sanctuary smelled of lemons and bleach, as though it had just been cleaned. The burgundy carpet still had the vacuum lines showing, and the gold on the chandelier lights sparkled, with crystals shaped like diamonds. Even the windows were clear, allowing the last of the sun to shine through.

Pastor Faircloth, a slim man, three inches below Terrence's six feet, entered the room wearing a black double-breasted suit. He either didn't wear a tie today or may have removed it prior to their arrival. His top collar was unbuttoned in a more relaxed look.

"I hope I didn't keep you waiting. Please follow me."

Neither had been in his private office before. It contained traditional wooden office furniture except for the Pastor's executive chair, which looked more like a throne. He had one picture of Jesus and a cross on the wall. The room was painted a serene blue and the only photo on his desk was of him and his wife.

Terrence and Casey sat in two hard-backed chairs that were well suited with the rest of the decor. He recalled the reason they were there and tried to tamp down his embarrassment. Why couldn't they be like other professionals that solved their problems without the need for counseling? Especially for such a sensitive subject. Resentment settled in.

Pastor Faircloth closed the door and took his seat. "I was surprised when you called asking for counseling, Brother Reed." His gaze quickly shifted to Casey. "I would've thought you two had a perfect relationship." Casey's dark brown eyes glazed over with ice.

"Well Pastor, I thought we at least had a good one," Terrence responded as he reached to hold Casey's hand. The Pastor's eyebrows shot up. Evidently, he didn't miss Casey sliding her hand away before placing them in her lap.

Pastor Faircloth's thick lips pulled into a disapproving frown. "Either one of you care to tell me what this is about?"

Casey's shoulders tensed, and she stayed silent.

Terrence sighed, "Okay, I'll start. Over the weekend, we went on an anniversary trip."

"Oh, that's nice," Pastor said, smiling, "A happy occasion."

"Well not so happy. We argued on the way. The next morning, I wanted sex, and she didn't," he confessed.

Pastor grimaced and shot Casey a look that she ignored, by meeting his gaze head-on with a disdainful one of her own.

"But he did it anyway," Casey blurted out.

"Now she's saying I raped her," Terrence concluded and folded his arms over his chest, hoping that was all the Pastor needed to hear in order to set Casey straight.

"Sister Reed, what do you have to say to this?" Pastor asked as he took off his suit jacket and rolled up his sleeves.

"What he stated is true," she replied, and her hands balled into a fist. "However, let's get something clear. I'm not just saying he raped me. I know for certain that he did."

Pastor glanced at Terrence, and they shared a look that let him know the Pastor was on his side.

"Now, Sister Reed," Pastor said in a patient tone. "You know the Bible. Even if you have an argument, you need to submit. Men have needs, and if the wife doesn't take care of them, another woman will."

Casey's smirk showed her loathing for the turn in the conversation. She gestured to the photo. "Is that why you're on your third wife? The woman you were sleeping with before you officially divorced wife number two, sir?"

"Sister Reed, that was uncalled for," Pastor snapped, a vein throbbing at his neck, as he looked to Terrence for assistance.

"Why are you attacking the Pastor?" Terrence asked. "He's only trying to help us."

"No, Terrence, he's trying to help *you*," she responded, sliding to the end of her chair. "This is where you get your ideas of how our marriage should work, but it's not working. Well, let me drop some knowledge on you and the good Pastor. The bible does say 'wives submit yourself to your husband.' But it also says, 'Husbands love your wives, even as Christ also loved the church, and gave himself to it.'" She pointed at Terrence. "Right above that scripture is another verse that says, 'submit to each other.' Below that scripture are two more that says the husband should love the wife as his own body, and that he loves his wife as he loves himself." She glanced at a stone-faced Pastor. "But you don't ever teach on that. Do you?"

Terrence could only stare at his wife, who locked gazes with him.

"If you treat me as less than my value, and are disrespectful, how am I supposed to uplift and support you? That's like co-signing on being mistreated." She put her focus on the Pastor. "You can twist that any way you want, but it doesn't mean I have to believe it. Your take on submission is all about putting the needs of one member of the family ahead of another. Terrence never did that, and I'd bet you've never done it, either."

"Casey, he didn't mean it that way," Terrence growled, turning to face her. "Calm down."

"Sister Reed, no disrespect," Pastor said in a tone he normally reserved for those not in his congregation. "But as the Pastor of this church, no one knows the Bible better than me."

"I'm sure you do, but that doesn't mean you can't misinterpret it strictly for your benefit, or for his."

Grabbing her purse from the back of the chair, she stood and headed for the door. She stopped halfway there and said over her shoulder, "You'll understand that my tithes will no longer be hitting your church's bank account." Casey pointed at the Pastor with a look that dared either man to protest. "Terrence, if you continue listening to him you won't have a wife." Her footsteps were brisk as she walked to the door. "By the way Pastor, what he neglected to tell you is that he likes going through the back door," she said, looking directly at the old man as Terrence turned to take in Pastor Faircloth's shocked expression.

"Last time I checked, sodomy was considered immoral and a sin."

Chapter 10

Casey was still in no shape to go to work the following week. She wasn't ready to deal with her patient's issues when she had some of her own to handle.

"Caring Hearts Counseling, how may I direct your call?" Irene's pleasant voice came through the phone, and it had the rasp of a woman who had been a two pack a day smoker.

"Good morning, Irene. Can you move my urgent cases to one of the other counselors? I'll pick up the rest when I return next week," Casey asked.

"I sure will, Mrs. Reed," was Irene's only response, but the hesitation in her voice showed she wanted to pry but wouldn't. Missing a single day of work was unlike Casey. Two weeks would definitely raise some eyebrows.

"Thank you, Irene," Casey said, ending the call.

Today, she just needed time to herself. Time to think, plan, and prepare for the future. Especially after that fiasco in Pastor Faircloth's office. The nerve of that man to think she wasn't smart enough to see through his bull. She'd peeped his game from the first day she sat in the pew. However, since she didn't have her own church affiliation anymore, she was only able to protest becoming a member for so long. Terrence was adamant that the children be raised in the church.

The first thing she had to tackle was to schedule an appointment with a psychiatrist. She scrolled through the contacts list until she found a familiar name. Denise Anderson, a woman she had met at a symposium on psychosis in Atlanta, Georgia.

During this first trip after grad school, Casey felt out of her league with so many seasoned professionals in attendance. Denise eased her nervousness with her colleagues by talking about their families and children. Then she broke the ice with several others. Denise also specialized in treatments for victims of rape, more specifically marital rape and domestic abuse, an area of practice with an increasing demand. Casey had referred a few of her clients, so she was well aware of the woman's effectiveness.

Denise was an advocate because she had spent a decade in an abusive marriage being repeatedly sexually assaulted by her husband. Back then, the laws were different. North Carolina laws prohibited a spouse from being prosecuted for rape. This didn't stop or deter Denise's efforts in getting out or helping women escape bad relationships. She even found love again with a wonderful man, and they'd been happily married for nearly thirty years.

After the fourth ring, Casey was sure the call would go to voicemail. "Hello, Dr. Anderson here," the friendly voice said.

"Denise, this is Casey Reed." There wasn't a need for a lot of preamble because she believed Denise already knew the reason for the call.

On the other end the sound of rustling papers came through the phone. "What can I do for you?"

"I need to schedule an appointment with you. Preferably after hours."

"Hold on one second, let me see what I have."

Denise was silent and several minutes passed before she came back on the line. "Did you ever get an assistant?" Casey asked.

"I had one, but she quit. Something about me being eccentric and antiquated. Not sure where that came from," Denise laughed, and it eased a little of Casey's tension. "Just because I don't do things conventionally and I still use a physical calendar doesn't mean I'm out of touch."

"But you have an iMac to help with all of that."

"I have the computer for work, I just don't see the benefits for me using it elsewhere. I can see you Friday evening at seven. All my clients will be gone. May I ask which patient this is about?"

"That'll be perfect. And the answer is me," Casey responded as she disconnected the call before Denise could ask the questions Casey wasn't ready to answer.

Having accomplished one thing on her list, it was now time to get Skye ready for school and TJ for daycare. She really preferred to keep them home but didn't want to upset their routine. After today's visit with her personal physician, she should be released from the doctors' care. She was almost certain that all the stitches had dissolved. There was only minimal tenderness, but it didn't mean that mentally she was ready for her normal life to resume. Slowly, she rose from the bed and made her way to her daughter's bedroom at the far end of the hall. Walking in the Disney-themed room, Casey found the seven-year-old in her closet looking for clothes.

"Good morning, Mommy."

Smiling at her beautiful daughter, Casey pulled the little girl into her arms. "Good morning, my sunshine. What are you looking for?"

"The My Little Pony shirt to wear with my jeans," she replied, as she returned to her search.

Casey walked to the dresser and opened the second drawer, extracting a pink t-shirt with the little white pony with blue dots and purple hair.

"This one?"

"Yes, thanks Mommy," Skye beamed.

She ruffled her daughter's curly hair as she bypassed the wooden chest overflowing with toys. "Finish dressing, princess. I'm going to get your brother ready." She turned to make her way to TJ's room at the same moment as Terrence walked out of the brightly colored nursery.

"What were you doing in there?"

"He was crying, so I checked on him," he said.

Both had entered the room fully now, with Casey picking up TJ. She pulled the diaper seam from his waist, peering inside for a quick moment.

"Really?" Terrence snapped. "He's my son. What do you think I did to him?" Fuming now, he grabbed her shoulder, but she brushed him off.

"I can't believe you think I'd harm my child. This stops today," Terrence said, punching the wall on his way out of the room.

Assuring her son was alright, she dressed him in a plaid jumpsuit and white shirt and went to find her husband.

When she walked into their bedroom and saw him sitting on the edge of the bed, she said, "I no longer know what you're capable of. Since you have a penchant for rear end action."

Terrence flew off the bed and stopped mere inches away from her.

"Okay, you are out of line. Way out of line. I know you're mad at me, but I would never, ever hurt Skye or TJ. For you to suggest otherwise is highly inappropriate."

As if summoned by her name being mentioned, their daughter appeared in the door fully dressed, tears streaming down her face. "Why are you yelling?" In full-blown seven-year-old hysterics now, Skye ran to her mom for comfort, wrapping her arms around Casey's leg.

Kneeling down to eye level she said, "Baby, we're sorry. We didn't mean to upset you." She wiped her daughter's face with trembling fingers. Once she was calm, she said, "Go wash your face."

Tension filled the air as the two stared each other down from their positions. Not one word passed their lips, but the heated glares could've set the house on fire. Casey went back to TJ's room to get him and his bag.

"Bye, Daddy. Mommy can we go, please?" Skye said, pulling on the hem of Casey's shirt.

"Yes, baby. I'm right behind you."

Terrence barely moved to allow her to pass. "I meant everything I said," he warned. "Your accusations went too far. Say whatever you want about me, but never, ever question the safety of my kids when they're with me."

"You're right," Casey agreed. "I'm sorry. No matter what's happened between us, I know you'd never harm TJ or Skye," she said before turning and walking from the room.

Chapter 11

Casey was eager to get back home once she dropped off the kids. Her first stop was to the doctor's office for a follow-up. A few moments after she signed in the nurse called her name.

"Casey Reed."

"Hi," Casey said when she was directly in front of a brunette who looked fresh out of high school. Time was passing so fast. Pretty soon Skye would be eligible for a job.

"Hi. This way, please. My name is Amber, and I'm assisting Dr. Perkins today," she said, leading Casey through a maze of hallways, smaller offices, and past an x-ray room. "Can you step on the scale, so I can get your weight?"

Casey placed her purse on a wooden ledge near the scale and climbed on the metal contraption. She thought about the many women struggling with trying to control or come to terms with the digits that were displayed on the screen. Thankfully, her weight hadn't changed much since TJ was born. She still weighed one hundred twenty-five pounds.

"We'll step into this room, I'll get your blood pressure and a few other vitals, then Dr. Perkins will be with you," Amber said.

Casey followed all of Amber's instructions, then watched as Amber keyed all the details into the laptop, laid out all the equipment, and pulled a gown from the bottom drawer of the table. "Please put this on, and the doctor will be in." "Thank you," Casey said, complying.

Five minutes later, a light tapping sounded at the door, causing Casey to snap out of the unsettling thoughts about the reason she'd come. "Come in," Casey said.

"Hi, Mrs. Reed. It's good to see you again. Before I start, how have you been?" he asked, motioning for her to sit in the familiar spot and pressing the button to call Amber back into the room.

"I'm fine, Dr. Perkins." She rose from the chair and sat on the edge of the table. "But I'll be better once you tell me everything's clear," Casey said, trying to make light of a heavy situation, just as Amber knocked and entered the room.

Amber helped Casey slide back and lay on her side. Dr. Perkins rolled the tray that Amber had prepared closer. Amber held her hands while Dr. Perkins checked the area. Casey's anxiety kicked in bringing with it the unwanted memories of the visit she'd had at the emergency room.

Your injuries will require several stitches. The doctor took swabs from the area around your nether region. All this information will be included in your rape kit. Casey tried not to think on those moments again.

"Okay, we're done. You're healing nicely," Dr. Perkins said, snapping off the gloves and tossing them into the trash can.

Amber helped Casey sit up on the table and closed the back of her gown.

Dr. Perkins stepped to the sink to wash his hands. "I removed that last stitch. Continue to soak in the Epsom salt for at least the next two nights, then you can go back to regular baths or showers." He dried his hands on the hand towels. "No sexual activity for at least another two weeks."

"You have nothing to worry about on that end. There'll be none of that for a very long time," Casey muttered.

"Amber can help you dress if that's necessary. Please let me know if you have any issues or concerns. Once you dress, you're free to go. I'll lay your papers over here."

"Thanks for everything, Dr. Perkins." He nodded and left the room.

"Do you need my help?" Amber asked as she stood to the side of the bed.

"No, I should be fine. I appreciate you staying in here and holding my hand."

"It was my pleasure," Amber said, smiling at Casey, trying to put her at ease.

* * *

The thirty-minute drive wasn't long enough to push the discontentment from her mind. She'd seen the inside of medical facilities more in the last month than she normally did in a year. On many levels, she was disappointed with Terrence, their marriage, church, and in some respects, herself. As she approached her house, her mother waved from the Lincoln parked in the driveway.

So much for resting today.

"Mom, what are you doing here?"

"Since I know you weren't at work today, I figured it was time for us to talk," Ella stated. Her tone was resolute, so was her facial expression.

"And just how'd you know I wasn't at work?" she asked, settling the purse strap on her right shoulder.

Ella's long legs allowed her to keep pace with her much shorter daughter as she answered, "Because I called, and that sweet Irene told me you weren't feeling well today." She paused and tapped her foot, waiting. "And I never got an answer Sunday about why you were walking funny. So, here I am."

Casey bought a little time to provide an answer by opening the front door and putting her coat in the closet before taking her mother's fur.

"Before you open your mouth to lie," Ella warned, sitting down at the closest place. "Please remember that I'm the one that knew you lied about sneaking out of the house to be with that lanky boy." Her voice lowered, "I'm also the one that knew you lied when you said your Uncle Dale had never touched you. You had that same defeated look in your eyes then as you do now."

Her mother was like a dog with a bone if she had questions and would continue gnawing at Casey until she got down to the marrow. Casey was tired of carrying around the weight of what happened alone. Now was as good a time as any to confide in the woman who'd made certain that her own brother had gone to jail over what he'd done to her daughter.

"Okay, something did happen on the trip." Casey sat beside goes her mother on the greenish-gray love seat. Ella purchased it for them when they moved into their first home. Casey had a feeling her mother loved it more, but since it wouldn't fit the décor of her home, she came to visit it every now and then.

Minus a few details, Casey explained the anniversary night.

"Honey, is that all? It was your anniversary. Why didn't you just give him what he wanted? You should be glad that you have a fine man like Terrence. He's a hard worker, takes care of his children, and he to church." She placed her hand on Casey's. "That's what's wrong with the younger generation. You don't appreciate a good man when you find one.

Casey stared, unable to believe that her own mother sounded more like Pastor Faircloth. "For real? If that's the case, I should've just let Uncle Dale do everything he wanted."

"Oh, that's different." With a wave of her hand, Ella brushed off the idea. "Hush with that foolishness. Your uncle was a pervert. There were warning signs that we ignored. Don't traumatize your children like that. You're overly sensitive because of what you've been through, but don't lay that in Terrence's lap. This man is your husband. There's an old record that says when you tell a man to scat, another woman's crooking her finger saying, 'Here, kitty.'"

Casey could feel her blood pressure rising. She cursed her mother in her mind but valued her life enough to never let the words flow from her lips. One thing Ella did not stand for was disrespect. The woman could slap someone so hard their skin would come clean off. Then she'd dare them to pick it up. She may be ditzy about some things, but she didn't play when it came to that.

However, this was different. The minor detail she left out shouldn't have made a difference but getting her point across made it necessary. "Give him what he wanted?" Casey repeated. "Tell me something, you let dad in your back door?"

Ella blinked, the understanding lit in her hazel eyes. She clutched at an imaginary set of pearls and said, "Oh my."

Chapter 12

Terrence's world was spinning on its on axis. After Casey left Pastor Faircloth's office that night, he spent hours trying to justify his actions to the man he admired almost as much as his grandfather. Then once home, he and Casey argued until she left the master bedroom and slept in the guest room again. In the morning it was more of the same. Now she was accusing him of the unthinkable with their children.

He entered the gym, ready to work off some frustration. Terrence dropped his bag in one of the steel lockers and jumped on the treadmill to warm up while he waited for his friend Blake.

Terrence increased the speed and the incline on the machine to accelerate his heart rate. As he ran, all he remembered was the heated conversation with Casey and Pastor Faircloth. Casey had never displayed that level of disrespect to clergy outright. Although she'd had plenty to say about him in the comfort of their own home. Now, she'd gone so far as to attack Pastor Faircloth about his wives, and to a man of God? She was losing it. How long was it going to take before things were back to normal?

When he got home, he was going to try and get through to her. Their lives had been turned upside down for something that wasn't even intentional. Now, because she had told too much of their business, the pastor was giving him the side-eye, but at least he was still on his side.

Terrence nodded as Blake, a tall man with a dark complexion and medium build entered the gym and headed toward the free weight area. Gradually, Terrence decreased the speed on the machine and lowered the incline. As his heart rate returned to normal, he brought the machine to a complete stop. Grabbing a towel, he swiped it across his face, then walked to the small area behind the cardio machines.

Blake caught the attention of every woman in the gym and a few men as well. He seemed oblivious either way, even of the ladies that tipped into the free weights area behind him.

"What's up, man?" Blake asked. "You ready to do a set?"

"Rack up two hundred pounds," Terrence replied, as he laid back on the bench.

Blake stared at his friend before asking, "Man, you serious? That's a lot of weight for you."

"Let's do this already. I need to let off some steam." Terrence lifted his arms to receive the bar.

Blake didn't move right away. "Alright, you need to talk about it?"

"Not right now, just hand me the bar."

Terrence realized Blake was eyeing him closely, probably because his veins were straining in his neck. At one point, Blake asked, "Did you just growl at me? Something's going on with you and I want to know what's up." Blake lifted the weights again as before, slowly placing the rod in Terrance's open hands. "That's too much weight for you. You're gonna pop a vessel," Blake warned.

As he lifted the barbell up from his chest, Terrence grunted.

"Let's do two sets of fifteen and switch off," Blake offered, without taking his eyes off Terrence.

Terrence continued lifting as if he hadn't heard him. Finished with his first set, he slid off the bench, so Blake could claim the seat and Terrence could spot him. Terrence struggled to stay mentally present in the workout session. Thoughts of last night continued to plague him. The way Casey described everything to Pastor Faircloth and took it out of context, he worried that the pastor would question his sexuality based on what Casey said. Bad enough that she had doubts, but he planned to squash that very soon. They needed to be back on the same page again.

As Blake finished his set, Terrence returned the silver bar to the rack and added another five pounds to each side.

Blake hesitated to claim the spot at the head of the bench. "An extra five is over your max." Terrence removed his shirt, ignored the whistles from the ladies and returned to the bench.

"Man, five more and that's the set," Blake said as he counted "five, four, three, and two… set. What are you doing Terrence?" Veins straining and arms shaking, Terrence continued.

"I said that was set," Blake snapped.

Lifting one last time, Terrence dropped the bar into the rack and grabbed his towel from the floor.

"I told you set a few minutes ago," Blake said, wiping sweat from his own face. "Are you crazy?"

Terrence kicked invisible dirt from the floor. "I'm just a little frustrated, that's all."

"Frustration or not, that's entirely too much for you," Blake said, "Unless you're trying to kill yourself." Blake ended their normal routine because Terrence wasn't focused and had made a move that could have strained him to the point where a hospital visit was on deck.

"It's not like Casey would mind if I did," Terrence mumbled.

Blake dropped down to the wooden bench and Terrence waited for him to bombard him with questions. His grandfather and Pastor shared the same stance. Somehow, none of their views were helping the situation. If anything, they made the situation more complicated because he kept trying to stay in their good graces and failed to make it into Casey's.

"Come on bro, talk to me. What's going on with you two?" Blake said.

He gestured for Terrence to follow him into the locker room, bypassing a few other guys who were dressing. Both took seats at the back, close to the showers.

"She's been tripping since we went on our vacation."

"How so?" Blake asked, still wiping sweat from his face and arms.

Lowering his voice so no one overheard him, Terrence said, "I was trying to make love to her, and she said I raped her."

"What made it different this time, considering you two have been together for a while? You do have two kids, it had to have happened twice. Did she say no?" Blake asked.

Terrence flipped over the scenario in his mind. "Well kind of."

"Kind of? Either she did, or she didn't," Blake emphasized, throwing his hands up.

Terrence rubbed his hands down his face as the image of the blood on that white material came to mind.

"If she said no, then you stopped, right?" Blake commented.

Terrence looked around a few minutes before he said, "It's not a matter of whether I stopped. I had previously suggested we do something a little different. She's not down with that, but she did agree to try something other than the missionary position. We were…um doing it doggy-style and while I was back there, I accidentally slipped." Blake's eyes widened.

"Now, according to her, I raped her and was trying to assert control."

Blake stared at Terrence as though he'd lost his mind. "Let me understand this," Blake said, rubbing his face. "Are you saying you sodomized your wife?" The words were loud enough that not only the four men in the room heard but probably a few outside.

"Dude, she's my wife," Terrence protested. "It was an accident, but Pastor Faircloth teaches that wives are—"

"Come on, I know you're not still listening to that idiot," Blake commented, his face a mask of apprehension. "I told you to leave that church the same time I did. He was becoming a fanatic then." Blake draped the towel over his shoulders and said, "No wonder you're frustrated."

"Pastor Faircloth is a man of God," Terrence yelled, drawing the attention of other men in the locker room, who eyed them with interest.

"You're talking about the old dude off Freedom Drive?" a sweat suit-clad man asked, stepping closer to the two.

"Yes. Why do you know him?" Terrence asked, frowning at the unwanted intruder.

The man, slightly taller and lighter than Blake, grabbed an Adidas bag and sauntered over to where Terrence and Blake stood. "Your church is not in your bedroom. Don't let your pastor cause you to lose your wife."

Before the stranger left, he looked back at Terrence as if he wanted to say more but shrugged and kept going.

Blake was back in Terrence's face. Evidently, he was determined to help him see where he'd gone wrong.

"I don't get how an accidental slip has become about rape," Terrence said. "She went to the hospital, the police questioned us. I explained what happened but refused to answer any more questions without a lawyer." Terrence noticed all the guys around them taking a lot longer than normal to dress and they were closer to them than necessary. "Why are you guys sticking your nose in my business?" he snapped.

"Man, you're the one in the gym putting all your business out there," one of the guys countered. "Don't blame us for you being stupid," he said, slamming sweats, shoes, and a towel in a bag. I hope she reported you, because they'll love someone like you in prison."

Terrence flinched at those words and took in the disgusted expressions on the faces of the remaining group.

"We hadn't been intimate since my youngest was born," Terrence explained to Blake. "It was always the kids, work, or she was tired. I needed to be with her."

"Did you apologize for hurting her?" Blake asked.

Terrence tried to remember the bulk of the conversations he'd had with Casey since that night. "Maybe. I can't say for sure that I did."
Blake scratched his head as if trying to reconcile this new revelation with the man he'd known for years. His eyes narrowed to slits. "Do you really love Casey?"

"Yes, man, I love my wife with my whole heart," Terrence replied quickly. "I don't want to lose her, but she won't let go of this thing." He remembered the look of disdain she gave him and the pastor, and his spine stiffened. "I'm not asking forgiveness for something I didn't do."

"Let me ask you this. Did she at any time tell you no?" Blake asked.

Terrence reflected on the scene from that night. "She just called my name, but I can't remember her telling me no."

A muscular young male, with a buzz cut and a marine tattoo pointed at Terrence. "If she was trying to get away from you and you didn't stop, you've raped your wife, dude."

Terrence looked at the younger guy, took in the boxing gloves he held, and took a few steps back. "It's still her word against mine. Even the media has blurred lines about what's considered rape in a marital situation. I know my rights as a husband." Terrence raised his hands in a defensive posture, as almost every man in the locker area backed him into a corner.

"Son put your hands down. They aren't going to hit you." An older gentleman stepped forward from the crowd. He looked to be in excellent health for someone sporting that much snow on top. "Do you know what happens to a woman when she's raped?" His thick British accent was a direct contrast to his complexion.

Terrence lowered his head, focused on the grey carpet, and said, "No."

"Well, that's alright because I'm going to tell you youngsters something," the man said, causing Terrence to look up at that point. He scanned the expectant faces of the men from all ethnic backgrounds. "When a woman has been violated, she goes through anger, depression, and she may isolate herself from her family. It destroys her trust, not only in the person that raped her, but also in everyone.

"Some of the men nodded, taking that in. Blake moved forward and asked, "How do you know all that?"

"Because I have a sister who went through a similar situation and it left her messed up mentally, physically, and emotionally." He turned his focus back to Terrence purposefully. "Some may try to take revenge on their attackers, and those are the lucky ones who even have that kind of mindset. When you take away her right to say no, you also take away her voice." He moved to the bench and motioned for Terrence to sit beside him.

"Mentally, she may no longer feel she has a right to say no to anything, or anyone. She'll blame herself and second-guess every decision she makes from that point on. Nothing will be the same in her mind." He scanned the faces of the men, as even more filed in and paused to see what was going on. "Ask yourself, would you want this for your mom? Your sister? Your daughter? I think not. Why would you do this to your wife? Your marriage license doesn't give you permission to assault." With that, he gave Terrence a parting look, before leaving him and the other men to think about his words.

This old man's message hit hard, and suddenly Terrence understood what an ass he'd been.

Sighing, Terrence lowered his head in his hands. "I screwed up."

The men spread out, resuming what they'd been doing before they gathered around. "What are you going to do about it?" Blake asked. "I can tell you it's not going to be easy to fix this."

After a moment, Terrence stood, he grabbed his towel, and headed toward the showers. "I need to talk to my wife and apologize for taking her to see Pastor Faircloth. Maybe I can set us up with a real marriage counselor. One she trusts."

Chapter 13

Adah went to the police station to speak with the detectives who took the initial call. She had uncovered some other avenues they needed to investigate. Instead of driving, she made the short walk over to Asheville Police Department.

She stepped into the station, the click of her heels signaling a woman on a mission. A light tap on the door was all she gave as she cracked it and awaited the invite into Chief Barry Hudson's office. "I need to see Detectives Winship and Jacobson, please."

Chief Hudson, a balding man with a round frame, and yellowish tan skin, the kind that comes from a can, gave her a once over. "Can I get a heads up on why you want to see my best detectives?"

Adah stepped close to his overcrowded wooden desk, "I thought I could save time by telling you all at the same time. I will give you this, it's concerning the possible rape they investigated a few weeks ago at Cedar Crest."

Chief Hudson picked up the phone and called the men into his office.

"Hey Chief, what's up?" one of them said as they walked in talking amongst themselves.

"Sit down, guys. The DA wants to see you." Hudson pointed at two seats in front of his desk.

"I understand that you guys investigated an incident at Cedar Crest Inn," she began.

"We did, but the wife isn't pressing charges," Detective Winship responded.

Adah sat on the corner of the desk. "I think this case is far more substantive. If I'm correct, I'll l be prosecuting the case with or without the wife's cooperation. I need you two to follow up on a few things. How did they meet? Past girlfriends and boyfriends? I want to know where they went to school, who their friends were. Uncover everything even down to the type of toilet paper they use."

Detective Winship scribbled on a pad, "Anything else?"

"Also, go to South Carolina and follow up with the wife and husband," Adah insisted.

"That's it?" The two paused for a response, and when there was none, they left the office.

Adah shook Chief Hudson's hand. With the severity of the wife's injuries, she doubted this was the husband's first time. In most of her other cases, the offenders were narcissists, sociopaths, or psychopaths, or a combination. These men needed power and control. In two of the other cases that landed on her desk, the wife made more money than the husbands. One of those husbands thought by demeaning her, it would make him feel more like the man he was supposed to be. He failed to realize his wife never saw him as less, nor was she worried about who made the most money.

She saw them as a team working together. He only saw himself and his ego, and it landed him ten years in prison. The other case didn't end as well. The husband beat the wife repeatedly. Several attempts were made to remove the woman and her child from the home. The day officers had legal grounds to take action, and with a request for a wellness check from the grandmother, they arrived to find all three of them deceased. The mother and child had been killed before the father turned the gun on himself. Adah planned to never lose another woman and child to domestic violence.

She made the short trek back to her office. Greg Wallace's words "They only pay me to defend him" didn't sit well with her. For him to resurface after falling so far off the grid smelled of corruption. The sooner she found who was behind the exchange of money, the better.

Chapter 14

After the unsettling and unexpected scene at the gym earlier in the day, Terrence returned to the comfort of his office. He made an appointment with an actual marriage counselor. He could've left this task to Casey but since he'd evidently caused the problem, he needed to provide a solution. If she wasn't comfortable with his second choice, he'd let her pick the next one.

Terrence dove into his work, trying to get his sales figures to line up accordingly. A tap on his door, interrupted his process. "Come in," Terrence beckoned.

"There are two detectives here to see you." Lela gestured toward her desk.

"Can you give me a few minutes?" What did they want to see him for? Maybe an employee had gotten in trouble.

"Sure, Terrence," Lela responded.

He paced the floor for a minute, trying to think. He was aware that Casey had spoken to the police, but that was in Asheville. He should've had nothing to worry about in South Carolina. Why was there a nagging doubt in the pit of his stomach?

When another soft rap on the door started, Terrence rushed to his seat, composed himself to appear calm, and said, "Come in."

Lela escorted the two gentlemen in, one clearly of a mixed heritage, the other one with a shiny bald head, as though he had just returned from active duty. "Sir, Detectives Jacobson and Winship." Each man nodded with the mention of their names. She slipped back out the door but gave the much older of the two a lingering look.

"Please have a seat, gentlemen," Terrence offered in a relaxed voice. "What can I do for you?"

"We're investigating an incident that took place in Asheville back in December." Detective Winship looked at Terrence with condemnation. "We need to ask you a few questions. If that's alright?"

Anger gave rise to the fear that had settled in his heart and for a moment he wished his wife had never planned that damned trip. First this thing with Pastor Faircloth, then with the guys in the gym coming at him like that, now this.

"Ask away," he said.

Detective Jacobson pulled out a pad and scribbled as Detective Winship said, "We need to know more about the events that led up to your wife arriving at Mission Hospital last month. You spoke with us at the hospital, but that information isn't adding up with the injuries she sustained."

Inwardly, Terrance cringed at hearing the words.

"Can you walk us through that morning step by step?" Winship asked.

"Why are you still investigating this? My wife said she wasn't pressing charges."

Jacobson placed his pen down before saying to Terrence, "We're trying to close our investigation, but we need your cooperation since you wouldn't answer questions at the hospital."

The detectives shared a look that Terrence couldn't decipher.

Terrence walked them through the night before and up until the moment they left the Inn. "I didn't know it was a crime to make love to your own wife."

"I have one more question," Jacobson said.

Terrence tried to keep his breathing even.

"Why didn't you accompany your wife to the hospital if it was just a little sex gone wild, like you said?"

"She left before I could get my clothes on," Terrence answered, kicking himself for not insisting on riding with her. "I wasn't sure she was actually going to the hospital or just being a drama queen. You know how women are."

Both detectives scribbled something on their pads, placed them in their jackets and stood to leave. Terrence followed suit, extended his hand to them and waited the brief seconds before they returned the gesture. "Thank you for coming gentlemen. I assure you that no crime was committed."

Winship smirked and Jacobson's expression was pure stone. "We'll be in touch."

Before they could reach the door, alarms went off in Terrence's mind. "So, you're actually pursuing this?"

"That's entirely up to the district attorney," Winship replied as they walked out of the office.

Chapter 15

Two weeks after she had the last of her stitches removed, Casey left the comforts of her home and went back to work at her cozy downtown office. The building was nestled between an antiques shop and the office of an accountant who seemed to never work, even in tax season.

"Good morning, Irene," Casey said as she grabbed the messages from her assistant's desk.

"Good morning, Dr. Reed." Irene glanced up from an open file. "I'm glad you're back. I'll bring your coffee."

Casey was happy to be back. Maybe dealing with her patient's issues would help keep her mind off her own situations. The practice was growing and had taken on two new staff members. Each counselor had been asked to offload at least one client to each of the new members. Part of her task today would be deciding which patient she could safely transfer, and if there were a few others that could be better served by having a fresh eye on their issues.

Irene tapped and entered the door simultaneously. "Here's your dark roast, ma'am."

"Thanks, Irene," she said after sipping the strong brew. "What did I say about calling me ma'am? I should be calling you that, not the other way around." Casey sat her cup on the coaster.

Irene gave her a stern look that spoke to every one of her thirty years as a teacher. "Nonsense. You're my boss, and I'm grateful for the job."

Her assistant sauntered her tall athletic frame out of the office and Casey made a mental note to start hitting the treadmill at home or take in some aqua aerobics' classes. Irene's venture into fitness was putting everyone in the office to shame.

Casey had nine clients scheduled for the day. Their issues ranged from marital discourse to bipolar disorder and schizophrenia. Noon slowly approached as Casey had wrapped up her third patient, a woman who suffered from depression, anxiety attacks and suicidal tendencies. Now that the woman no longer posed a threat to herself, only a few more maintenance sessions remained.

She noted all the charts, transferred files to the new therapist, then sat in the office, thinking over everything that had happened between her and Terrence. Had she been so busy over the last eight years that she didn't notice the change in him? He'd become more sarcastic and demanding, almost callous, but she thought it was because he was stressed out about work. How could she miss that it was a part of his makeup, and Pastor Faircloth was only feeding his need to have control.

Casey thought about their wedding day on February 14th, eight years ago. Tears fell from her eyes as she remembered how much love was shared. So much hope that they would be a successful, loving, happy family.

Casey covered her face to hide her tears, becoming so distraught, that she didn't notice Alex Baxter slide into her office. Alex was not only one of the partners in the practice, but he'd been her best friend since their days at Graham Middle School. The two of them had been inseparable. Rumors ran amuck in high school that they were a couple, but that wasn't true. Except the one kiss they shared on a dare, they had never crossed that line. They made a pact before graduating that if neither married before thirty, they would marry each other. Right before her twenty-ninth birthday she had met Terrence and fell in love with him. Alex on the other hand, found a woman he considered to be his soul mate and thought they'd be together forever. That love produced a handsome, energetic, nine-year-old son, Jordan, who Casey adored as if he were her own.

"What's wrong?" Alex asked, reaching to guide her from the executive chair. He wrapped her in a pair of sturdy, muscular arms that bolstered her in a way she sorely needed. As she breathed in his woodsy scent, she relished the warm and comforting feel of him. Seconds later she remembered where they were and moved back, putting some distance between them.

Casey grabbed some tissues from her desk to wipe her eyes, trying to avoid looking into his.

"I was walking to my spot and saw you crying," he said, his handsome face reflecting concern. "I just wanted to make sure everything was alright with you."

"I'm fine, Alex. Thanks for checking on me." Casey shook off those melancholy feelings and took in all that was Alexander Baxter. He really was a handsome man, about 6'3", muscular build, and brown eyes that held the warmth of a slow simmering fire. If she got too close, she would be singed from the embers. His chiseled chest alone caused her heart to flutter, and lord those thighs ... have mercy. If Terrence wasn't her husband, things may be different. Sometimes she regretted that the pact had said thirty. Twenty-five would have been better all around.

"You're far from being alright." He entered her space. "This is me. You can tell me anything."

She stared at him and contemplated spilling her secrets. "Alex, I —"

"Dr. Reed, there are two detectives here to see you," Irene said through the intercom.

Casey took a breath, almost wishing she hadn't told them to meet her here. Their presence was going to make others have questions. "Send them in please."

"Alex, can you excuse me please?" she said taking in his curiosity. "This is a very private matter."

"Alright, I'll go. But I'm here if you need me;" he said giving her hand a gentle squeeze."

"I know," she whispered.

Alex whisked past the detectives. One with bronze skin and sapphire eyes, and one with chestnut skin and hazel eyes, strode into the room eying Alex with pointed interest.

"Detectives, thanks for coming," she said leaving the desk to close the door behind them.

Taking a seat and removing his hat, the one with the eyes deep enough to swim in said while he extended his hand to her, "I'm Detective Winship."

Casey shook his hand before glancing briefly out of the window and watching the birds land on the telephone cables.

"I mentioned that we wanted to follow up with you on the incident at the Inn. We've already received statements from the B&B owners, as well as the SANE nurse. The DA sent us down to speak with your husband and you about that night."

Casey put her focus on the detectives and said, "If you have statements already, why are you here?"

The detectives shared a glance, before the hazel-eyed man said, "Detective Jacobson," but didn't extend his hand. "We wanted to see if there was anything you wanted to add?"

"I never said I was pressing charges," Casey responded, suddenly alarmed at the fact that the incident was getting way more attention than she anticipated.

"Since I didn't give you any statements initially, I would assume I have nothing to add at this point." Casey placed her elbows on her desk. Personally, I'd like to let it go."

"It's not that simple. The DA said that the State may want to pursue the case, with or without you pressing charges."

She thought about what this new situation would mean. Only a few people knew the details and given the fact that even her own mother brushed off her accusations, she wasn't sure if she was ready for so many people to be scrutinizing her life this way.

"Adah Osmani, the prosecutor in the case, will be calling you once we turn everything over. After that, Mr. Reed will officially be charged and taken into custody."

Detective Winship stood and both men moved toward the door. "We've taken enough of your time. If we need anything else, we'll be in touch."

"Thank you for ..." Casey blinked as something came to mind. "Wait, did you say Adah Osmani?"

Winship answered with his hand on the door, "Yes I did. Why?"

"I was given her card by the owner of the B&B. I've looked at it several times debating on calling. How much time before you think all of this happens?"

Detective Jacobson looked at his partner. "Maybe two weeks, tops. Why do you ask?"

She sighed, feeling a sense of doom. "Just needed to know when my life is going to implode."

Chapter 16

Casey never worried about Terrence becoming physically violent, but he was not above manipulating anyone to get his way. If the cops were thinking of arresting him, she needed to make sure she and the kids were far away from the house.

Staying with her parents was not an option, especially after the last interaction with her mother. She'd been avoiding phone calls ever since. Her father would side with Terrence as well. He believed a man was the head of his castle and that women were to clean, cook and take care of the children's and their husband's needs. Not exactly in that order. Her mom had tried on several occasions to reestablish the career she'd abandoned when she married Phillip. Her father threw a major production to show things were so bad without her being in the home that she quit after several attempts and finally gave up trying.

Casey called her other best friend, Marla, who could be counted on to always have her back. Friends since college, Marla was a drop-dead gorgeous woman who had legs for days, and a figure that would make a super model jealous. Her high cheekbones and flawless complexion had all the guys chasing her in college, including a few professors who almost landed on the wrong side of tenure when she said, "Yes."

"This is Marla Davenport. May I help you?"

Casey left her desk and lounged on the sofa. "Hey, lady."

"I'm sorry, who's calling? Is this my bestie who hasn't taken my call since her anniversary?"

"You play entirely too much."

"Girl, I'm fine, but what's up with you?" Marla said, with all playfulness gone from her voice. You don't sound good. Do I need to check ol' dude?"

"Put your blades away woman." Marla had never been a Terrence Reed fan. She considered him a blood-sucking parasite. Then when he tried to keep Casey from her friends, he fell even lower in her eyes.

"I do need to ask if the kids and I stay with you for a while."

There was only a slight pause. "You know you all are welcome anytime. Should I wait to press you about what's going on?"

Casey crossed her legs and laid her head on the cushion "I promise I'll explain everything when we get there. Later, girl."

Chapter 17

Breaking down in the office was bad enough. But the fact that Alex caught her falling apart and then saw the detectives who showed up, was more than she could handle today. She was certain there would be more questions from the detectives as well as from Alex. At that moment, she said a silent prayer in the off chance that Alex found out what Terrence had done. He would kill him for sure. Alex, like Marla, had never cared for Terrence, since that night he made her wait an hour on the side of the road when her car had broken down on the way home from work. All to prove a point that she shouldn't be working late.

She grabbed her purse and laptop bag from the drawer. With her blazer in hand, she was on her way out the door. Her appointment with Denise was only twenty minutes away, but navigating the rush hour traffic, the movie crowd and those folks who were coming in from work as well would make it almost an hour.

Dr. Anderson's office was the perfect blend of eccentric and medieval times--a perfect extension of Denise's adventurous personality. Her education had given her the understanding that choosing certain colors and artwork was a way to provide a sense of calm for the patient. At this moment, Casey felt the opposite of the emotion the décor was supposed to inspire.

Her family always said that only crazy people saw head doctors. Which meant they'd been sorely disappointed in her choice of career. *"We don't run around telling everyone our business. We deal with our own,"* Casey's grandmother always said.

Truth is, her family just ignored the schizophrenic and bipolar characteristics when it came to Uncle Ryan, Cousin Robert's talking to "extra people," and Aunt Betty's severe bouts of depression, because God forbid, they admit those things weren't "normal."

The words "Casey Reed" were said in such a formal tone that they sounded foreign coming from Dr. Anderson's mouth. Even though this was Casey's colleague, she had never visited her on a professional level. She'd heard Dr. Anderson speak on topics that ranged from psychosis in the workplace to the lifelong effects of childhood sexual abuse. She came highly regarded by peers and patients alike. The fact that she would be discreet was essential.

"Please come this way." This time the warm, mellow voice was more like normal and belied her six-foot-plus stature. "You could've come through the back door, you know." Dr. Anderson said looking over her black framed coke bottle glasses. "Even though I usually have no patients at this time, next time I'll have you come that way."

As Casey ran through several ways to get to the heart-of-the-matter, when she took a seat on the chaise, she hesitated, trying to form the words that had become a daily part of her existence: my husband raped me.

Seconds later, she took the coward's way out. "I can't sleep at night"

"And why is that?" Dr. Anderson asked, resting her ivory hand on the arm of a plush chair and locking her gaze on Casey.

Putting her focus on the antique clock, Casey mulled over the new internal dialogue that now stayed in the back of her mind while doing housework, taking care of the children, consulting with patients, speaking with her peers. Because she tried to push it all away, every time she wrote out a case report or rubbed a crying patient's back, and even something as simple as placing an aspirin on the tip of her tongue—the memory danced in the corner of her mind like a shadow chasing the footsteps of a ghost.

Casey looked the woman she'd known for ten years straight in the eye, saying, "My husband raped me."

Dr. Anderson placed the yellow pad on the rustic table between them. Her thick eyebrows arched with concern. "I could see how that would keep you from sleeping. Have you considered asking him to leave the house, or have you made any other effort to separate?"

Casey removed some tissues from the box of Kleenex on the table in front of her because she was sure the water works were coming. "I've considered both. I'm planning to go to a friend's house with my kids when I leave here."

"My first task is to make sure you're safe. Do you need protection getting you and the kids to your friend's house?" Dr. Anderson reached for the phone at the edge of her desk. "I have someone on call who'll be waiting for you when you leave and will make sure you arrive."

"No, I don't think that's necessary." Casey folded her hands in her lap. "He wouldn't hurt me or the kids."

"You know as well as I do that in these situations when a man feels he's losing everything, his reactions are not normal."

She thought that over for a few moments. Terrence did have a temper, and he'd become even angrier lately. "That'll be fine. Thank you, Dr. Anderson," Casey said, pressing a tissue to her face.

"Don't thank me yet. Let's sort out the damage this has done to you. Do you feel comfortable enough to tell me everything?"

Casey stretched out on the chaise, bracing herself to share. Dr. Anderson picked up the yellow notepad and jotted down some things the moment Casey uttered her first word. The only pause came when Dr. Anderson asked questions to clarify points.

"I sleep a little, but every little sound in the house wakes me up. I've been a light sleeper since the children were born, but now I could hear a ghost tiptoeing on marshmallows." Casey laughed a little at her own joke. "I'm on edge, grumpy, and unable to concentrate on my clients."

Dr. Anderson walked over to a bookshelf while Casey continued talking. "I've heard of cases where patients with PTSD have heightened senses, and it sounds like you're there." She returned to her seat and handed Casey a book titled *The Courage to Heal*. "Don't read it yet." Dr. Anderson placed her hand in front of the book before sitting back in the chair.

"I want you to bring it to each session and we're going to work through it. Casey, have you been intimate with Terrence since this occurred?" Dr. Anderson questioned.

Casey shivered with disgust. "I can't stand for him to touch me."

"You know the normalcies for the process. Don't think it changes because you've become the victim." Dr. Anderson walked to her desk, pulled out a pre-typed prescription pad, wrote out a medication and signed her name.

"This will help you sleep. It's very low dosage. I want to see you again in a week. Don't worry, Casey. We can definitely work through this."

Chapter 18

After picking up her kids from school and daycare, Casey pulled up to Marla's house. This was going to be a long night. Explaining to her friend what was happening in her marriage would probably cause the woman to break out the knives. When Marla got angry that's the first thing she reached for. Although she'd never cut anyone, she had threatened many. She'd mellowed out since then, but this might send her into those old ways.

Marla opened the door and rushed toward the car. "Hey, my babies. Oh my gosh, you two are getting so big."

Skye giggled at her comments, while TJ continued blowing bubbles, fascinated by his own spit.

Stepping into the arms of her friend, she felt foolish for being afraid to tell her what had transpired. As astute as Marla was, she probably already had an inkling that things weren't well between them. She'd been kind enough to keep it to herself.

"Let's go inside and get the kids settled, then we'll have some tea and talk. Unless you need something stronger."

"Stronger would work." Casey grimaced. "About eighty proof." Both grabbed a bag and walked in unison toward the house.

Marla had purchased the single level ranch home in the Ballantyne area through a short sale. The spacious living room with a sunken floor and fireplace was immaculate. The white plush carpet was not something Casey would have with her kids, but it was beautiful for a single woman. Working in tandem, they got the kids fed, bathed, and dressed for bed. Thankfully, after a bedtime story, they were out. Skye didn't even bother to ask about her daddy. Marla was her favorite person in the whole wide world, so it might take a minute before her eight-year-old mind realized something was off.

Marla heated the water to pour them both a cup of African Autumn tea on her stainless-steel stove. As she pulled down the porcelain cups, the citrus scent of oranges and cranberries filled the air. "Tell me what he did," Marla demanded, cutting through the silence of the house. "You're loyal to a fault and the only thing that would have you running away like this would be if he did something reprehensible. So, talk."

Casey moved from the island, past the table. First, she started with other things that had transpired in their marriage. Like the incident with her being on the side of the road, or having to carry his bills for a month, and the things with Pastor Faircloth. Then every detail of an anniversary gone wrong, even though she knew this would make Marla hate him even more.

"Now you know why I left tonight," Casey said over the rim of her cup. "I couldn't stay in the house with him any longer."

"Well, technically with what he did to you, he should've been the one to leave, not you, and never the kids." Marla stepped from the stove to the island with the tea pot. She replenished Casey's cup.

"Mar, I know but I'll try to work that out in court if I decide I want to stay there."

Marla stood at the island watching her friend twirl her cup. "This is going to court?"

"Two detectives were in my office earlier," Casey replied, still shocked that the DA was pursuing this. "The same ones who were at the hospital asking questions." She stood to get a refill, only this time she opened the cabinet, pulled down the black rum and poured a generous helping.

Marla took a seat at the table and crossed her legs. "How soon are we talking about?"

"Within the next two weeks if the Prosecutor moves forward."

Casey joined her friend at the table. "I have a question for you. Why do you still hate him so much?"

Marla looked away and shrugged. "Girl, you know me."

"Yes, I do. That's why I'm asking what he's done that made you hate him so much?"

"You forgot that I knew him way before you came to campus," Marla began. "I watched him manipulate people the whole time he was there. Thinking that his suave ways and good looks could get him any girl. Some of them even did his assignments. Girl, he wasn't that bright. He knew how to use people, even the teachers." Marla stood and just poured straight rum in the cup before taking a long swallow. "I just always felt that you sold yourself short with him. Other guys at the University were more deserving of your time, but you loved him, and since I love you, I supported you."

Marla cleared the cups, honey, and lemon from the table. Casey was deep in thought, taking it all in, and wondering how she, who considered herself pretty observant, missed all of that. Marla was correct on some levels but not in the fact that he wasn't deserving of her.

"It's not that I didn't know my worth," Casey said. "I just never set anyone beneath myself. I've always tried to start all my acquaintances on an equal playing field. Maybe I was just more focused on getting my degree and starting my practice than I was being worried about what Terrence or any other guy was doing." Casey stood. "Since all of this happened, I've felt that I never knew him."

The silence between them was only broken by the slight hum of the dishwasher before Marla said, "Look, it's okay. You don't have to figure everything out tonight. Why didn't you press charges immediately? He needs to be in jail, and that's the truth."

Casey paused, thinking of the answer she would give. "He's my husband," she said.

"He's still guilty of a crime and should be sitting in a six by eight cell," Marla fussed.

"I went to the hospital and the nurse did a rape kit." Casey relived that invasive process for a moment, including when she first stepped up to the triage window. "I had five stitches and she said that it could all be used for evidence if I decided to press charges against Terrence. Apparently, she wasn't aware of the law and neither was I. The decision on whether he's prosecuted has been taken away from me."

Marla moved to stand and there were only a few inches between them. "How'd you leave this out of our earlier conversation? At no time did you say that you'd been to the hospital, or that you had stitches." Marla opened the drawer and pulled out two knives. One a bowie that had a wooden handle with grips perfect for nimble fingers. She'd once told Casey how she loved the cold feel of the steel blade and that it was heavy enough to do damage. The second one, heavy braided steel all the way down with jagged edges. She walked into the living room and grabbed her keys and jacket from the coat rack.

"Where are you going?" Casey asked, trying to keep up with her friend.

"To your house to have a little chat with your husband," Marla replied opening the door.

"You can't do that, because you'll be the one to end up in jail." Casey grabbed her hand, pulling her back in. "Please let me handle him. That's why I didn't want to tell you in the first place. You always overreact."

Marla stood at the door huffing and glaring at Casey before she laid the weapons back down. "Fine, have it your way. I won't terminate his life, but I still plan to have a nice long conversation with him."

Casey let out a long, slow breath. "I'm going to check on the kids and go to bed. I can't take any more drama today."

Chapter 19

Detectives Winship and Jacobson left the precinct and traveled to the University of North Carolina at Asheville to follow up on a lead they garnered from some old files they found. As they walked into the admissions office, a tall, lanky guy with thick glasses and a pocket protector was the first person they encountered. He took in both gentlemen and frowned as though he knew they were law enforcement and he was the one in trouble. "Can I help you?"

"Actually, I think you can," Winship said, stepping up and leaning on the circular wood desk. "We need to find student records."

"You're at the right place," he replied before saying, "Follow me."

They walked down the hall past the restrooms and the director's office, into a room with two laptops, one large mainframe, and tons of files. At the first laptop he came to, he signed in and looked up at the detectives.

"What's your name?" Jacobson asked.

"Grant, Grant Borders. Who are you looking for?"

"We're searching for the last known whereabouts for Brittany Weaver."

Grant's hands paused on the keys. "I'm not supposed to give out information like that. Can I ask what this is about?"

Detective Jacobson pulled out a subpoena. "You can ask, but this is all you need to know."

Grant gave the legal document a good once over. He pecked at the computer for a few minutes then scribbled on the back of the document and handed it back to Jacobson. "You could've just mailed this." "Well, we need this in a hurry," Jacobson stated.

"She left school after one semester and never returned," Grant said and shrugged. "She dated my boy, Terrence. I'm not sure what happened, just know she left suddenly."

"What do you mean suddenly?" Detective Winship inquired, sliding to the edge of the chair he pulled up.

"She went home for spring break. Then I heard that her dad and uncle were here packing her stuff and looking for Terrence. Except Terrence hadn't returned to school yet. The last known address we have is on that paper. It's in Georgia."

Winship scanned the paper Grant handed him. "Looks like we're going to Georgia."

Jacobson said, "One more question. When was the last time you saw Terrence Reed?"

Grant frowned as though pulling his information from the recesses of his mind. "At his wedding. About 2010, I think."

"Great. Thanks for your help." Jacobson said as they walked back out the way they came. Before he got to the car, Winship dialed the district attorney.

"DA Osmani, how may I help you?"

"Winship here. We got an address for an ex-girlfriend. Seems like something strange happened. It's in Georgia so three-hours from South Carolina and back."

"Good. See if you can find out more about her relationship with Terrence."

"We're on our way."

Chapter 20

"Marla, the kids are fed and in bed. Can you keep an eye on them?" Casey asked the next evening as she realized that the stay with Marla would be longer than a night.

"Where are you going?" Marla inquired.

"I need to go by the house and pick up a few things before Terrence gets home from work."

Marla left the sofa and grabbed her purse. "You aren't going there alone. We'll just have to take the kids with us."

"I'll be fine. Put your purse down and stop overreacting." Casey maneuvered past the love seat and headed toward the door. "I'll return within the hour."

* * *

Casey went through the familiar spaces in their house and gathered everything she thought she'd need over the next few weeks. She paused to trace her hand over one of the pictures on the fireplace. She remembered vividly when each one was taken. From their wedding photos to the birth of the kids and every Christmas since Skye had been born. Happier times.

"Those were good times, weren't they?"

Sudden movement in the room made Casey's hand freeze on the last picture they had taken together. "What are you doing here?" she demanded, kicking herself for staying too long.

Terrence said, "I live here. And you?"

Casey's eyes flickered to the bags then back to Terrence. "I came by to get a few things, then the pictures caught my attention. But I'll be leaving now."

Terrence stepped closer, invading her space. "Why'd you do it, Casey? We were working things out."

She moved until she was flush against the fireplace. "Do what? I don't know what you're talking about."

His expression darkened, eyes narrowed to slits. "Why'd you press charges against me?"

"I didn't do anything," she admitted. "The DA doesn't need me to press charges."

Terrence was so close, she could smell his stale breath. "It still comes back to you. If you hadn't gone to the hospital, none of this would be happening."

Casey closed her eyes against the anger that rose to the surface. She shoved Terrence with all her might. "Wait one minute, don't try and blame this on me. All of this started because of you and your control issues. If you're pointing fingers, start with yourself." She moved around him to grab her bags and run.

Terrence grabbed Casey's arm, then slammed her against the fireplace so hard she couldn't breathe. "I'm not finished talking to you."

She tried to snatch away, but his grip held her in place. A muscular arm came out of nowhere and grabbed Terrence by his collar, lifting him off the
floor.

Casey slid to the carpet.

"I suggest you let the lady go," came a familiar voice.

"Alex, no." She managed to get to her feet, stumbling as she moved forward until she was facing Alex. What she saw in his eyes was frightening.

"Casey." He didn't take his hold or his gaze off Terrence. "I need you to get in the car."

He didn't have to tell her twice. Casey's breathing returned to normal as she sat in Alex's car. She was thankful that he appeared when he did. She had believed, albeit foolishly, that Terrence wasn't a threat to her or the kids. She understood that he was stressed about the whole situation, but he needed to take ownership of what he'd done and stop blaming everything on her.

Alex left the house, his steps eating up the pathway, approaching the car in high stride before she could catch her next breath. "Why'd you come here without anyone to assist you in getting your things?" he snapped. "I'm trying to wrap my head around why you thought that was a good idea." He said all of this before his rear end hit his European leather seats.

"He was only trying to frighten me," Casey responded, noticing his swollen knuckles and wondering just what had transpired when she left them alone in the house.

"He seemed to be doing a good job of that when I walked in." Alex pushed out a heated breath as though to steady his rampant emotions.

Casey rubbed his knuckles. "Did Marla call you?"

"No, she didn't." Alex relaxed as her smooth hand rubbed over his.

"Let me walk you to your car so I can follow you to Marla's."

"How'd you know I was here?" Casey asked, remaining in place.

Alex sighed. "Can we go somewhere and talk instead?"

Alex used his index finger to lift her chin. "Everything will be alright, I promise," he said.

"Drive to my house and we'll talk there, if that is acceptable."

"Okay." She opened the door and sprinted to her car. Casey called Marla while en route and let her know she'd be there in about an hour or two. Marla ensured her the kids were fine before asking, "Are you alright?"

Concentrating on the road, Casey responded, "For the most part. I'll explain later when I see you," and disconnected the call.

Alex motioned for Casey to pull in one of the three garages attached to his Victorian house located on a few acres of land near Lake Norman. He made sure her car was parked inside and left his on the outside. Casey loved the house, especially the spacious kitchen. The stainless-steel appliances sparkled from the light shining down on them.

Alex walked her to his cozy living room. The hues of brown gave the room a sense of warmth. "Please have a seat."

Casey settled on the supple leather loveseat. The deep chocolate color went well with the gray cashmere walls, giving the place a masculine feel. "Where's Jordan?" Casey asked.

"He's with my parents for the two weeks over winter break. I go over and spend a few hours with him each day after work. Stop stalling. Tell me what's going on between you and Terrence."

She looked him in his eyes and said, "I left Terrence and I've been staying with Marla."

"Does this have something to do with why you were crying in the office?" Alex asked.

She didn't respond because he already knew the truth.

Lowering her head, she sighed. "I wasn't going to tell you, but you'll find out eventually."

"There's been a sadness in your eyes for the last six months. It hides behind your smiles, but it's still there when you think no one's watching you."

"Even though you're my friend, I couldn't tell you what happened. Now that it's going to be in the news, it doesn't matter who knows.

Terrence is going to be arrested and charged with rape and assault." Casey folded her hands and, placed them on her lap.

Alex frowned. "Do you know this woman?"

"I do …" Casey said, averting her gaze. "You're looking at her," she said with an elaborate hand gesture.

Alex focused on her face and realization dawned in his dark brown eyes.

"What?" he grimaced. "Why that slimy mother—"

Casey stood. "Alex, stop. It's not your problem. I have to go back to Marla's." She took her purse and headed toward the door. "Wait, you never did say how you knew I was at the house."

He hesitated a few moments. "Remember Denise telling you someone would make sure you made it home safe?"

"What does that have to do with you?"

"Some of her clients are in volatile situations, so I've been helping in that capacity. Since I followed you that night, I've been kind of watching you. You work late all the time and I wanted to make sure you were alright. I wasn't aware that the person you needed protection from was already in the house. I need you to decide. Either you stay here, or I'll drive you to Marla's house. I don't want to risk Terrence lurking somewhere, waiting to hurt you again. Then I'd be going to jail."

"Look, I appreciate the offer, but I think it's best that I go to Marla's. You can follow me if it makes you feel better."

"We're only talking about you sleeping here for one night, not staying the rest of your life." Alex stepped within a breath of her lips. He held up his hand to silence her. "I'm not trying to break up your marriage. Seems like Terrence is doing a great job of that all by himself."

Casey couldn't believe that she was freaking out about spending one night at Alex's house. And why was he so close he could taste the chocolate lip gloss she wore? With a reserve she wasn't aware that she even had, she took two steps back. "Please, let's go," she said breathlessly.

"Sure." Alex placed a chaste kiss to her forehead that caused her knees to buckle and pulled her into his arms.

Casey felt so loved being in Alex's arms. Instead of feeling the hardness of muscles, she felt softness with him.

Not another word passed between them as he escorted her to the car.

She arrived at Marla's, made it to the door and waved goodbye.

After finishing her bath, she couldn't wait to slide into the bed. She'd ignored the thirty texts and phone calls from Terrence. Each voicemail and text were even angrier than the last. They had nothing to discuss.

She didn't realize how tired she was, but sleep was a long time coming. Sometimes she would have the same reoccurring dream that carried snippets of that time in Asheville. She tried to fill her mind with happier thoughts. The last one before sleep overtook her was the desire she saw in Alex's eyes.

Chapter 21

Terrence cowered in the interrogation room of the Mecklenburg County Jail awaiting his attorney's arrival. Shortly after Casey and that meddling Alex left, two deputies arrived to pick him up for questioning. There was no way in hell he was spending a night in jail with common criminals for a crime he didn't commit. As soon as he was released, Casey and his gramps could expect a phone call.

"Officer, my phone call. And my attorney should already be here." Terrence said, holding the wooden desk as if it were a life preserver.

"The phone call will probably come before the attorney, because the one your grandpa hired for you had second thoughts," the young officer replied. His pubescent face looked as if he could still be in grammar school. "He found out who your grandfather was and said he wasn't suffering the consequences if he lost your case. Apparently, your grandfather has another one on the way. He should be here within the hour. I'll let you make your phone call in about twenty-five minutes." The officer walked away, speaking to one of the detectives that had arrested Terrence.

The detective entered the room where Terrence was already seated.

"Relax, we only have a few questions for you." He took a seat at the table opposite Terrence, a manila folder in his hand. "The faster you answer, the sooner you can get out of here."

"Whatever, I have nothing to say until my lawyer arrives," Terrence replied.

The portly detective opened the folder. "Just one question, then I'll leave you until your lawyer comes. If this one even shows. What happened between you and Brittany Weaver?"

The heat drained from Terrence's face, as the officer grabbed his folder and left the room.

As he closed the door, he said, "Bingo."

Chapter 22

Casey's phone rang, startling her from her sleep. "Hello".

"You have a collect call from Terrence Reed. Will you accept the charges?"

She was fully awake now because this was the first night without pills where neither a nightmare nor the kids woke her. "I guess."

"What did you do?" He growled. His tone spoke of barely contained anger.

"Why are you calling me collect?" Casey slid from under the cover, then flashed to his original question. "I didn't do anything. Where are you?" Casey asked, standing near the window.

"I was questioned tonight for assault and first-degree forcible rape," he snarled. "Get me a fucking lawyer."

Her blood boiled because he was accusing her without even knowing if she had pressed charges. She had told the officers repeatedly she didn't want to. Somehow, he expected her to jump to his bidding when he'd been acting clueless since the incident happened. Terrence needed to learn that the laws of God and the laws of the land were entirely different things. "Well, I guess you shouldn't have wasted your free call on me." With that, she disconnected the call.

Casey threw her phone on the bed as she screamed, "The nerve of him blaming me."

Marla ran into the room with a Louisville Slugger in her hand. "What happened?"

Her shoulders relaxed. "I'm sorry, I didn't mean to wake you. Terrence just called from jail. He's mad because he's being questioned again."

"Jail? I thought you said a couple of weeks," Marla replied, clearly still thinking someone was in the room as she paced, bat gripped firmly in her hand, checking out the scene.

"Would you put that down? There's no one here. The detective never said it would happen tonight."

"Well, there's nothing to do about it right now so let's go to bed and deal with it tomorrow." Marla covered a yawn.

* * *

Casey followed her normal routine the next morning, only giving Terrence and his rude phone call a minimal amount of thought. Once she walked through the doors of her practice, it became her haven. In fact, she looked forward to the daily exchange with her clients. Keeping an open line of communication was advice she gave her patients, but she couldn't seem to do the same in her own marriage. It was comforting to have someone appreciate even the smallest thing. Someone who didn't take people for granted and think everyone was put on earth to serve them. That's exactly what she received from her clients, gratitude. It wasn't about the praise, but everyone deserved at least a thank you every now and then.

She had been sitting at her desk going over patient files for the better part of an hour when she remembered that maybe she should call the detectives and find out more about the case. Before she could lift the handset, Inez buzzed her on the intercom. "I have District Attorney Adah Osmani on the line for you."

Seconds later, Casey stared at the phone as though it had offended her. "Thanks, put her through."

"Hello Mrs. Reed, I wanted to let you know we've had your husband at the precinct since last night for questioning."

"I'm aware of that," she said glancing at her wedding band. The ring sparkled, almost accusing her. "I'm not sure why. It was my understanding that I needed to press charges before you could arrest him."

"The fact that there was sufficient bodily injury gave us probable cause. I hope you'll agree to testify, because that will strengthen the case."

This confirmed what the detectives told her. "What happens next?" Casey asked.

"He'll be formally charged and arraigned later today. The judge will decide when the case will go to trial and if he can make bail. If you decide you want to press charges," the persuasive, composed voice articulated. "I'll need to take your statement of the events on that day."

"What time is the arraignment?" Casey asked.

"Today at 1:00 p.m.," Adah responded.

I'll be in touch when I decide. Thanks for calling, Mrs. Osmani." With that, Casey disconnected the call.

Then she called the one person she knew would go with her anywhere. "Can you meet me out front of your building at 11:00 a.m.? Terrence's arraignment is today."

"I'll be there," Marla said.

Several hours later, they were in front of the Asheville Courthouse. It didn't take long to find the courtroom, nor to lay eyes on Terrence, who was in handcuffs. His public defender was only slightly younger than dirt, pot-bellied, with greasy black hair, and sweating despite the fact that the air was cool. If the man made it through the length of the trial, she'd be surprised. Terrence's laser glare pierced straight through her, but Marla angled her body in front of Casey to block his view.

They took a seat behind the prosecutor as things got under way, listening intently as the DA read the charges.

Terrence's attorney was quick to yell not guilty once the judge asked how his client pleaded. With bail at one hundred thousand dollars, he'd be out before the sun set.

"Where will he get that kind of money?" Marla asked as they sat on the hard bench.

"That's pocket change. He has that in savings."

"You have it," Marla corrected. "Remember you make more than he does. Better put a lock on that cash before he drains it."

"Never thought about that. Let's go," Casey said as they walked out of the courtroom.

"Do we need to get the kids?"

"No, I swallowed my pride and called my mom. Since she loves her grandkids, she said yes. You can stop laughing now," Casey said drily.

"I'm sorry," Marla said between giggles. "It's just that I could see her reaction when you told her what happened, and then you accused your father of doing the same thing to her. How long did it take for her to slap you silly?"

"All of three seconds." She reached up and rubbed her cheek. "I can still feel it."

Marla parted her lips to respond, but Casey swatted her friend on the behind to shut her up. "She made me grovel, but she surprised me and apologized as well. She told me she loved me and that she was proud of me, and she'd always be in my corner."

"You know Ms. Ella don't play," Marla quipped. "Trying to act grown with her, please. I'm glad you apologized though. Now let's get some dinner and figure out your next steps."

Chapter 23

Casey woke gasping for air and soaking wet. She sat straight up in bed waiting for her heart rate to decrease. After establishing where she was, she made quick work of changing the sheets and stepped into the shower. She dreamed about killing Terrence and that thought shook Casey to her core.

While showering, she said a prayer for herself, for Terrence, and the kids to get through this. Not that she was thinking of rekindling her marriage. They had been a long way from happy, even before the anniversary weekend.

Desperately wanting to leave the house before her friend woke up, she slipped into her clothes, grabbed her purse, headed toward the front door, and ran right into Marla.

"Good morning," Casey said. "I have to go." She stepped around to make it out the door.

Marla blocked her path. "Good morning, I'll bet. Why the rush? Come have coffee with me. And a bagel or muffin."

"I can't really," Casey insisted. "I need to go pick up the kids."

"Why are you so nervous?" she asked with a wink. "Cause you think I'm going to question you about Alex following you home the other night?" She grinned. "Girl please, you're grown and if I was going to ask, I would've asked you that night. Besides, I know you wouldn't do anything with him while you're still married to your asshole of a husband, even though it would hurt him as much as he has hurt you."

Turning to face her, Casey said, "I was at the house getting stuff for me and the kids and Terrence showed up."

Marla tensed, her head tilted as she scanned Casey, probably looking for signs of injury. "He didn't do anything to you, did he?"

"He grabbed my arm and was yelling at me. He blamed me for bringing the cops in on this. He believes I pressed charges against him. Then Alex showed up."

"Please tell me he kicked Terrence's butt."

"I have no clue what he did, because he made me wait in the car," she said as she slid into a seat at the table. "I noticed his hand was swollen when he touched my face. I wanted to know how he knew I was there."

No longer smiling, Marla asked, "And he said?"

Casey left her spot and grabbed the orange juice from the fridge. "That my therapist asked him to do it. As a favor to her."

"It seems we're both worried about your safety, because you certainly aren't."

"Why on earth would you say that?" Casey asked, reclaiming her seat.

"Because after everything he's done to you, you still haven't pressed charges. Only you and God know what he's done over the past eight years. What will it take? For him to hurt one of the kids?"

"He wouldn't hurt the kids. I've already had this argument with him," Casey bellowed.

"Just like he loved you, but he still hurt you." Marla placed her hand on Casey's shoulder. "I know it's hard because you really love this man. You have to think about the fact that not only did he commit a crime, he violated your trust."

"I know what he did," she whispered. "But I don't want this playing out in the media and my kids being damaged by this. Skye loves her dad very much. I can't imagine what this is going to do to her."

"Casey, kids are resilient. You're a counselor and I believe if something does go wrong, you'll pick up on it right away. Parents always think they are protecting their kids, but usually their actions have the opposite effect and they do more harm than good. Stop worrying and handle your business."

"Alright, I'll talk to her after school today. Now, I need to get moving. I have to stop by the district attorney's office."
"You're doing the right thing, Casey."

Chapter 24

Casey sat in her office thinking about the last several months of her life. Everything was off track now, except her practice. She mulled over her choice to implicate Terrence but realized so many people thought she was a basket case because Terrence was only telling his side. She reached into her wallet and pulled out a card that was wearing along the edge.

"DA Osmani. How may I help you?"

"This is Casey Reed. I want to come in and tell my side of the story."

"Really, what made you change your mind?" Adah said, sliding up to the edge of her seat.

"I wasn't ready, and I'm still second guessing myself, but I have questions and I think I should say something."

"When can you come in?" Adah questioned.

"I'll be in your office on Friday. I need to reassign some cases, but I can get there."

"Perfect, I'll see you then." Adah hung up the phone.

Content with her decision, Casey went back to her patients. She'd already had appointments with patients who had major depressive episodes, one with a bipolar disorder, and a paranoid schizophrenic. All of that was before lunch.

Terrence's upcoming trial was going to be a circus. Terrence refused to accept a deal that would quickly put an end to everything. The DA had offered a plea deal, but he would spend eight years in jail and have to register as a sex offender for the rest of his life. Couldn't see his own children. Terrence, through the defense attorney he hired, was still essentially claiming his innocence.

She hummed an R&B tune while thinking of what to have for lunch. Casey's mind drifted to Alex and everything he'd done over the past few months on her behalf. The biggest smile she'd been able to manage for weeks appeared on her face.

Why am I sitting here acting like I'm Cherelle singing 'Things I Miss at Home,' all because this man showed me an ounce of affection? "Nope, not going to happen."

Her heart fluttered and as if on cue, the man himself was standing in her doorway. She couldn't deny that she was attracted to him. If truth be told, she always had been. Alex was a distraction, but nonetheless one that she didn't need. Her life was already a fickle mess. She was grateful Alex respected her enough to let his wishes be known and to give her time to sort things out.

"Hey, I was just running over to Nana's to grab a bite to eat. Do you want anything, or do you want to come with me?"

Casey prayed she didn't have the lovesick puppy look on her face. She felt like a teenager with her first boy crush.

"Let me grab my purse." She didn't miss the fact that he was smiling. "Instead of Nana's, let's just go to the café across the street since we both have clients an hour from now."

"Sounds good to me."

Alex stepped back so she could leave first. She wondered if aside from being a gentleman he was enjoying the view of her backside.

The lyrics of Cherelle's song still echoed in Casey's head as the pair walked in silence across the street and entered the café. The restaurant wasn't enormous but seated a nice business crowd at lunch time. Usually the place was bustling with people, but this was a good time for them to come. Now they could talk without having to shout over the noise. Alex led Casey to a table for two in the corner and pulled out a chair for her. He placed their orders of meatloaf, mashed potatoes, cabbage, and a yeast roll, then returned to his seat across from her.

"How's it going?"

"I'd assume you already know since you've been assigned as my personal body guard." Casey batted her lashes before breaking out in a smile.

Alex laughed. "I see you've got jokes today. It's good to see you in a jovial mood since you've been kind of distant lately."

"Well, let me see you go through everything I have going on and remain intact."

"Easy, I meant nothing by that other than it's good to see you smile. Look, I'm sorry. I'm just very concerned about you. I don't want what you have going on at home to affect your work here with your clients. You're very good at what you do, but you haven't been mentally present in this office since you came back from your vacation months ago. Your patients haven't noticed because they're a little self-absorbed. You've been pacifying them, but the staff has noticed that you're not at your usual standard."

"Have I really been absorbed in my own world?" Casey asked, her gaze darting to the door that opened as a group of women entered for lunch.

Alex touched her shoulder, sliding his chair a little closer and saying, "It's not about what you have or haven't been. It's about making sure you're alright or if you need some time off to deal with what you're going through."

"I'm good," she said, ruffled that the rest of the staff knew she was off her game. "I also don't need the staff in my business either."

Casey pushed her chair back at the exact moment that the waitress came up behind her with their food. Dishes crashed to the floor, splattering their meals to the tiles.

"I'm so sorry," Casey said, remorsefully. "I didn't know you were behind me."

The waitress didn't say a word but gave Casey a sympathetic look.

Alex stood, and touched her on the arm, gently guiding her to her seat. "Please bring us the same order to go, and I'll pay for the damages and both lunches."

The waitress nodded and sped off.

Casey covered her face with trembling hands, more embarrassed than anything.

Upon seeing her so distraught, Alex reclaimed his seat next to her. "Hey, what's with the waterworks?" he asked. "It's okay. Once the food comes, we'll go back to the office. Go to the restroom and wash your face."

She was up in a flash.

When she returned, their food was on the table and Alex assured her he had handled everything. "You ready?"

"Yes, thank you."

"No problem," Alex said, as he stood and hugged her tight.

The door chimed, and as they parted, she met Marla's curious gaze.

She hoped that look was only an assumption of the way things appeared. "Hey, Marla."

Marla stopped in front of them. "Hi. I stopped by the office and they said you walked this way with Alex." She arched her eyebrow at Casey. "What's going on?"

"Nothing," Casey rushed to answer. "I had a minor mishap with the waitress and Alex took care of it. I was hugging him for buying lunch and paying for my mistake."

"Alex." Marla tilted her head toward him.

"Hi, Marla. How are you?" he asked, grinning.

"I'm well, thanks for asking."

"Good to hear," Alex said after an awkward moment. "Why don't I leave you two alone to talk? I'll take our food back to the office and you can eat it later. Unless you want me to leave it?"

"No, that's fine," Casey said, trying to avoid Marla's probing eyes.

Alex smiled, tipped an imaginary hat, and gave Marla a parting smile before moseying out of the café.

Chapter 25

Detectives Winship and Jacobson arrived in Georgia in just under three hours, pulling up to a white house with a long wooden porch and black shutters. It even had a wooden swing on the porch. The blinds were all drawn shut, and the grass needed to be mowed. Jacobson tapped on the door and waited. After what seemed like forever, a woman with a mahogany complexion opened the door.

"May I help you?" The age lines on her face mirrored that of an older woman, and the droop of her shoulders made her seem exhausted.

"Detectives Winship and Jacobson. We're looking for Brittany Weaver," Detective Jacobson said.

"I thought the case surrounding my parents' accident was closed?" the curvy woman said.

"This has nothing to do with your parents. May we come inside?" Detective Jacobson gestured toward the living room.

"Can I see your badges, please?" She glanced over her shoulder as a young boy moved forward and peered out at them.

She examined their badges and stepped aside so they could enter. The boy, who looked to be nine years old, walked over to Brittany taking a protective stance in front of her.

"Did you finish your homework?" she asked.

"Yes, Mama."

"Okay, I'll get your dinner."

"Excuse me for a moment. Please have a seat," Brittany said as she left the room for the kitchen. Her son followed her but glanced back at the detectives with a scowl, that made Detective Jacobson smile.

The smell of fried chicken, and turnip greens made Jacobson's mouth water. He, unlike his partner, was from the South. From the scent, this young woman knew how to throw down when it came to the kitchen. She returned with two glasses of sweet tea and handed them to her guests.

"You said you wanted to talk to me? I'm listening." She took a seat across from them, crossing her feet at the ankles like a church girl.

"Ms. Weaver, do you know Terrence Reed?"

She froze. Someone less experienced would've missed that, but not Winship. "I haven't heard that name in a long time. Yes, I know him."

"We understand that you tried to press charges against him. Is that correct?" He already knew the answer. She didn't try, she actually had.

"That was over nine years ago. Why are you asking me this now?" Her eyes volleyed between both men, awaiting a response.

"There's another case and the district attorney found your case file and reopened it."

"And what does that mean for me? By now, the statute of limitations has run out," she replied.

"It seems your case was dismissed with prejudice, so the DA can still press charges. Even after all this time."

"Mama?" Her son peered cautiously from the doorway to the dining room.

"I'm alright. Go on and eat," she said with a wave of her hand.

Turning back to them, she said, "The college didn't want to do anything, and the cops acted like they didn't believe me. I left school and transferred to the University of Georgia. I checked back a few times to see if any headway had been made in the case. The last time I called, there were no DNA results, and the detective retired all of a sudden."

The two didn't want to seem incompetent, but they had no prior knowledge of another detective on the case. There hadn't been any notes or results in the system "We apologize on behalf of the department,"

Jacobson said. "We have a new DA and we plan to get it right this time." "What do I need to do?" She tucked her hair behind her ear.

"Can you be in Asheville by Friday for a deposition?"

"I think I can. I just need to notify the school and get my aunt to keep my son."

"We'll get out of your hair," Detective Jacobson said, getting to his feet. "Here's our card. Please call once you're in town and we'll take care of your lodging and meals."

She took the card, opened the door and watched them leave.

On the walk to their SUV, Detective Jacobson glanced at his partner, and said, "That little boy looks mighty familiar, doesn't he?"

"Sure does."

"Someone in Terrence's family had some serious pull to make this disappear."

"The DNA wasn't available? That's bull."

"We need to find out about the detective who worked her case."

Detective Winship called the one person who was waiting on this news.

Chapter 26

"So, this is awkward," Marla stated, her focus remaining on Alex's retreating form.

"Do you want to tell me what's really going on between you two?"

"I told you what happened already," Casey said. "But since you think it's something else, why don't you tell me what it is?"

"Follow me," Marla said, dragging her to a table in the back of the café. "If Terrence had walked in and seen you hugged up with Alex, what do you think would've happened? You know it's not about if there's anything happening, as much as it would be about perception. Knowing how petty Terrence is, don't give him any leverage to try and get the kids from you. You're blind if you can't see that Alex has feelings for you."

"None of that matters. We're colleagues and friends. And besides, I'm still married, unfortunately," Casey said under her breath. "I take my vows seriously."

"Your marriage vows are not in question. Your husband could be on his way to jail for a long time. You're playing games with a man who obviously desires you. I don't think he'd cross that line either, but why are you baiting the trap?"

Casey stared at the waitress who was picking up dishes one table over, before turning her eyes back to Marla. "I have spent my life trying to be the good daughter, the dutiful wife and a great mother, for what? Is it so bad to want the one who's concerned for me, the one that's not afraid to put me first? I hate to think that if I hadn't gone away to college that Alex and I would've been married."

"Do you have feelings for him?" Marla asked staring down the ladies at the next table who seemed intrigued by their conversation. Casey arched her brow at her friend.

The ladies eavesdropping at the next table gawked at them and made a fast exit out of the door. Casey and Marla shared a laugh.

"I'll admit being attracted to him, but he's my best friend. My feelings are all over the place. I'm still sorting out all this mess with Terrence."

"That's what I needed you to understand," Marla said. "You can't play with other people's feelings just because yours are muddled."

Frowning, Casey said, "Maybe I want to pursue something with Alex. I definitely don't want to close the door. Now, why'd you come here looking for me?" she asked before flagging the waitress down.

"Two coffees, please," she said to the blonde waitress. This one was younger than the one that had waited on her and Alex.

"Coming right up," the young girl said, her voice as perky as her walk.

"Any news on when the trial starts?" Marla asked.

"Very soon. The jury selection begins Monday."

The waitress brought their coffee and asked, "Would either of you like sugar or cream?"

"Cream only, please," both responded in unison. "Thank you." They waited for her to leave the area before picking up their conversation.

"Enough about me, what's been going on in your life?" Casey asked.

"Since you're diverting, nothing's been going on in my life. It's obvious that you don't want to talk about this any longer. So, let's head back to work," Marla said.

"I love you, and thanks for being here for me." Both stood, and Casey laid money on the table, before they walked out the door.

"Casey, I love you too. I should've been there more and perhaps you wouldn't be in this situation at all," Marla replied when they stood on the sidewalk. "I'll see you at home later. Remember what I said. If you really want a relationship with Alex, don't play with his feelings. Wait until this situation clears."

She returned to work and made a mental note and physical effort to curtail her interaction with Alex. She was so thankful for Marla. Life had gotten in the way, but their friendship remained strong. Her grandmother always said, "Good friends are like stars. You don't always see them, but you know they're always there."

Chapter 27

Casey almost forgot that she'd scheduled a session with the pastors at her new church. She had attended a service with Marla the first weekend she moved in and wanted to give the new place of worship a try. Since the episode with Pastor Faircloth, she was a little skeptical of ministers who offered counseling services. But when she met the Tuckers, they seemed like genuinely good people. Her parents had even started attending regularly and had nothing but great things to say about the ministry team.

When she arrived at the massive red brick building, she wished she'd just opted to see First Lady Tucker alone. She wasn't sure she could make it through this session with the trial looming. But the need for a sense of peace and closure was important. It was the only way she could move on with her life.

"Come in," said Reverend Henry Tucker. His 6' 5" frame towered over the oak wood desk. "Please, have a seat." He gestured toward a blue chair that looked out of place in the enormous sanctuary. The dark circles under his eyes made it seem as if he had missed several days of sleep. First Lady Harriet Tucker's salt and pepper hair held more of its natural color than Reverend Tucker's full-on white.

"How are your kids doing?" he asked, taking a seat on the gray love seat beside his wife.

"The kids are well. Skye's very inquisitive and TJ's developing his own personality."

"That's a good thing. Now, how can we be of service to you this evening?" Reverend Tucker asked.

She told them everything that happened from the incident until Terrence was arrested.

"First, I want to say that for you and Terrence to have any chance of healing your marriage, you must be willing to give him a chance. While I realize that trust must be earned, you must present him the opportunity to earn your trust again," Reverend Tucker challenged.

"I don't think I can forgive him for what he's done. No man that loves his wife should ever treat her with such disregard. Why doesn't he even realize what this has done to me? What if I can never forgive him?"

Reverend Tucker stared in her eyes as he said, "Daughter, forgiveness is not for his benefit. Your healing is locked up in your ability to forgive. You must forgive him to release yourself. He will have to atone for his own sin. Do you feel that you bore any part in Terrence's actions?"

Casey couldn't believe Reverend Tucker was peddling the same stuff that Pastor Faircloth had tried to drop in her lap, only in a different way. Her fist clenched as more words came from his mouth, victimizing her all over again.

First Lady Harriet stared at her husband of fifty years, her expression registering disbelief. When he stopped speaking, she cleared her throat and said, "Henry, may I speak with you in private for a moment?"

The couple stepped outside the office for several minutes. When they returned, he addressed Casey. "I apologize to you because I never meant to patronize you. I was merely trying to determine if it was a misunderstanding or truly a violation. Please forgive an old man for neglecting your heart."

"I appreciate your apology," Casey said as she watched Reverend Tucker close the door behind him.

Lady Harriet patted the seat beside her and waited for Casey to join her. She enveloped Casey in a pair of loving arms.

She accepted the comfort and consolation she didn't get from her own mother when the incident first happened. Her tears flowed, and she cried for the young girl who was molested by her uncle. She cried for the sad state of her marriage, and the woman raped by her husband. The man who repeated the same atrocities he was supposed to protect her from. She cried until she was empty.

"How's it been for you since the incident?"

With a heavy breath, Casey spoke her truth. "I left the bedroom because I wasn't comfortable with him being there. I kept worrying he would do something else while I was sleeping, so I left the house."

"Baby, I understand your feelings," the first lady said as she continued holding Casey. "I can't justify what he's done to you, and I can't apologize on his behalf. Only he can atone for his sin. My concern's only for your healing and that you feel God's love for you right now. Even though you aren't ready for this, at some point down the road you will be. I want you to always know that you can feel safe and loved here."

Casey moved away from Lady Harriet, wiping her face with the tissues she was given. "Thank you. I wanted to walk out when Reverend Tucker was speaking. He was saying the same stuff I heard from my former pastor. I didn't buy it then, and I'm not buying it now. Somehow, I caused my husband to treat me with disrespect? I married him because I loved him and thought he loved me. But this has left me questioning everything and caused me to even doubt that God loves me."

Taking her hand, Lady Harriet said, "Now, I'm going to pray for you and your marriage. I want you to continue to pray that God will lead you in the path He desires for you."

Chapter 28

Terrence held tightly to his semi-permanent position in the living room recliner, drinking a beer, pissed at the world and himself. His boss told him it would be in the best interest of the company if he took a leave of absence pending the outcome of the case. He didn't want to face all the stares and murmurs of his peers, so he had agreed. Even with the many years he'd put into that place, management didn't offer any support.

The unrelenting pounding on his door was rankling his nerves. He wanted to wallow in his sorrow and not be bothered. He sat the bottle on the glass coffee table with no coaster, snickering because Casey would've been so upset by that. Since she was no longer there, he didn't give a damn.

He opened the door but when he saw who was on the other side, he threw his arms up in surrender and staggered back to his seat. "Ahh hell, why'd you come here?"

Percy Reed entered the room larger than life—Stetson hat, cowboy boots and all. Terrence never understood why his grandfather always wore that getup. It sure wasn't because he had an inferiority complex. Percy stood at five feet eleven inches, but his booming voice didn't fit with the lean frame that housed it.

"Boy, I just came to check on you."

"Gramps, really. I don't need this from you right now." Terrence ran his hand down his face, the stubble nearly scratching his hand. "Do you want a beer?" Terrence walked in the kitchen before his grandfather could reply. He popped the top and handed him a cold one as he sat back down.

"It's okay. The new attorney, Khalid Hassan is expecting a call from you. You're going to be fine," Percy said, handing Terrence a card. "You just need to stick with your story that you were just trying to love your wife."

Terrence took the card and slapped it on the table next to the remote.

"You weren't trying to hurt her. You got it?" Terrence nodded.

"Work on getting you a better deal, a lesser sentence."

There was no way he'd survive a stint in a cell. "Gramps, I'm not trying to be someone's girlfriend in jail."

"So, you like giving but not being on the receiving end?" Percy roared so hard with laughter he snorted and choked on his beer.

"Whatever, man," Terrence said, taking a swig.

"Now that she's gone, you can move over to my place. We'll fight that child support and anything else she wants from you. I told you she wasn't good for you." Percy took a hefty swig of his beer, stood and pulled out his checkbook. "Maybe we can offer her some money and make this whole thing go away."

Annoyed, Terrence glanced at his grandfather, as though truly seeing him for the first time. And what he saw made him recoil.

"You can't throw money at every problem, Gramps."

His grandfather snorted and settled back in his chair. "Since when?"

* * *

The banging out front had Terrence running to the front door. "Why's everyone coming to my house right now? I haven't had this much company in three years."

Terrence opened the door and on the other side stood two people he'd have preferred not to see. Theron and Arleen Reed stared back at him. A surprise because they hadn't been to his house in ages.

"What brings you two here? You haven't visited since Skye was born." He stepped aside so they could enter.

"We came to see how you're doing and because I need to talk to you, son. I've been trying to tell you for years, but you wouldn't listen because he was always in your ear," Theron said.

Just like a cockroach that always appeared when company came, Percy poked his head around the corner. "Well, look who's here," he taunted.

"I should've known you would be here. I'm surprised you haven't moved in," Theron said.

Terrence's head volleyed between his father and his gramps.

The tension in the room went from zero to one hundred in a millisecond.

"Theron, calm down. We didn't come here to argue with Percy," Arleen interjected.

"Tell him, Percy. Why you never liked Casey and why you've been waiting for her to leave."

Theron stood face to face with his father. They were the same height, but Theron outweighed Percy by at least a hundred pounds.

Terrence had turned the television back on to try to distract them from the argument that was certain to come.

"I'm your father, and you will respect me." Beads of sweat pooled on Percy's forehead once he removed his Stetson.

"Respect is earned, not demanded," Theron shot back, causing Percy to flinch. "You've tried to turn my son against me all his life because you didn't like Arleen. Instead of fighting you, I just stopped having anything to do with you." Theron addressed Terrence next. "Son, instead of cutting you off when you left home at seventeen, I should've stood by you, helped you make it on your own. Then his money wouldn't be so appealing."

Sensing that things were about to get ugly, Arleen glared at the two men. "Terrence, come to the kitchen and help me bring in drinks for everyone. Now." To the men having the standoff in the middle of the living room she said, "You two work this out while we're gone."

"No, ma'am. I think I'm going to stick this out."

"Terrence!"

"Sorry Mom. My house, my rules." Terrence hugged his mom. "I didn't like following rules at your house, so I moved in with gramps. We all know there were no rules where I was concerned."

Percy went in as soon as Arleen stepped out of the room. "We wouldn't have a problem if you didn't let that one lead you around by your—"

"That's my wife," Theron snapped. "Don't you dare talk about her like that." He closed the distance between him and his father. "She and I are a team. That's something you know nothing about. If you did, Mom would've never left you."

"That's a lie," Percy snarled, his fist shaking.

"Actually, I should thank you," Theron continued. "I learned how to treat my wife by watching you treat yours the wrong way for all those years."

Percy threw his hat on the table and got in his son's face. "Bull, your mom left me for another man."

"Keep believing that lie," Theron countered, standing toe-to-toe with Percy. "I know exactly why she left because I went to see her before she passed away."

Percy staggered backward. "What?"

Terrence remained rooted to his spot in shock. There had always been so much tension between his father and grandfather, but neither one of them would ever explain why. Now it seemed like a cork had been ripped from the bottle of their lives and the hurt, anger and family secrets were spilling out of their own accord and no one could stop them.

"She told me everything, father," Theron said bitingly. "So, either you tell Terrence how you planned to break up his marriage from the beginning, or I will."

Stunned, Terrence turned to the man who had raised him. "Gramps?"

Percy ignored his grandson and instead directed his wrath at his son. "You'll tell him no such thing," Percy growled, angling his body toward Theron. "Everything I did was for that boy, so he wouldn't be ruined by some woman like you'd been. So, he wouldn't make the same mistakes you made by being led around by the nose by some simpering woman with an inferior family that would never be good enough for a Reed man."

The sound of glass shattering caused everyone to look toward the door to find Arleen standing there with a stricken expression on her face and her hands free of the tray she had been carrying.

Theron turned a triumphant gaze to his father. "Congratulations, father," Theron spat the word like it was poisonous to him. "You managed to hurt yet another person who didn't deserve it."

Somehow, Terrence found the strength to propel himself forward. He stopped short of his grandfather and stared him down as if he were a stranger, not the man who had given him everything … and had just taken it all away. "Gramps, what have you done?" Terrence said in a voice of barely controlled anger. "You set out to ruin my marriage from the beginning? To break up my family and risk sending me to prison?"

Percy's eyes drilled a hole through Theron before turning back to look at Terrence with a vein throbbing at his temple. "I was just helping you, boy. I didn't tell you to rape her. You did all that on your own. I'm just trying to help pick up the pieces."

Arleen let out a gasp. "Rape? Terrence!"

"I didn't rape her," Terrence roared to no one in particular. "It was a horrible accident that I regret more than anything in my life. I'm looking at losing my family, and my marriage because I made a huge mistake," he said turning his attention back to his grandfather. "But the biggest mistake I ever made was believing in you."

"Now wait just a minute," Percy said puffing himself up to his full height. "All I've ever done is love you and try to help you."

"Help him?" Theron scoffed. "You wanted Casey gone so Terrence would come and take care of you." Theron turned to his son. "Terrence, your grandfather has prostate cancer and only three months left to live. He doesn't want to die alone. That's why he's done everything he knew how to disparage your wife, and to drive a wedge between you so that your marriage would fail. You would be devastated, and then come running back into his waiting arms. Then he'd have you right where he wanted you—until the day he died."

Deep down inside, Terrence knew what his father said was the truth. He recalled his grandfather's many invitations over the years, despite the fact he was happily married. "It's true," he said in a voice hoarse with emotion.

He turned to his grandfather. "Every heartache I've ever had has been because of you. My fractured relationship with my parents, my jacked-up way of thinking about a man's place in the home, my turning my back on Casey, my not being able to see my kids," Terrence choked out. "All of it because of your venomous influence."

"That's enough," Percy thundered. "For once, stop being a sniveling baby and take responsibility for your own life and for the decisions you make." Percy's expression was filled with disgust. "Do you honestly think I could've made you do all those things if deep down you really didn't want to? Grow up, Terrence. If your life is a disappointment, it's because you made it that way, not me."

Betrayal rolled around in his stomach like bile. He couldn't believe his grandfather would do this to him. "I've lost my job, my family, and possibly my freedom because of your hold over me. I gave you love you didn't deserve and the only thing you knew how to give back was control. You ran my parents off, tried your best to destroy every loving relationship around you, beginning with my grandmother. And for what? To feed your ego? Your sick, twisted idea of love?"

Terrence shoved his grandfather away. "Get out of my house," he said through clenched teeth. "I no longer want or need your help. And I certainly don't need your brand of love in my life. Stay away from me and my family, Percy Reed."

Shaken, Percy reached out to Terrence, but he stepped back. "Boy, don't be like that. I've protected you and made stuff happen for you all your life. We can fix this, I promise."

"I believed everything you told me, but now I'm done. I don't want to ever see you again."

Percy stood for several moments staring at Terrence's face. He turned to his son and daughter-in-law but found no sympathy in their eyes either. He'd lost. He grabbed his hat and set it back on his head.

"Fine, have it your way, but don't come groveling back to me when you realize your mistake." He eyed Terrence with barely restrained anger. "I'm telling you now, boy, if I walk out that door, I'm not ever coming back."

Instead of answering his grandfather, Terrence strode to the front door, opened it, and waited.

With an exclamation of frustration and rage, Percy stormed out the door. He never looked back.

Terrence slammed the door behind him, then took a moment to compose himself.

Arleen nudged Theron forward. "See to him," she whispered. "I'm going to clean up this mess."

Nodding, Theron walked over to Terrence, touched his arm. When he received no resistance, he turned him and enveloped him in his arms.

Terrence stood ramrod straight for a few moments, before he relaxed into his father's embrace. "I'm sorry," Terrence said in a raspy voice laced with pain. "I ... I've ruined every relationship I've had with the people I care about the most. Just like he did."

"It's okay, son," Theron said, clasping his son tightly. "I'm as much at fault for letting him do it, and for not fighting harder not to lose you."

Terrence battled the tears threatening to overtake him. Eventually, they won out and his body shook as they spilled, out wetting his cheeks.

Arleen rushed to their side and joined in the hug. She rubbed her son's back and whispered, "We love you, Terrence. We always have. Despite everything. Never forget that. We are always here for you. No matter what."

A few moments later, Terrence drew back. He wiped his face with the back of his hand. "I'm so glad you're here."

His father nodded. "Terrance, we can't remake the past, but we can make sure we change the future. If that's what you want."

Terrance glanced at his parents. So many years of loss. His entire world had just imploded from the inside out. Suddenly, he was exhausted, emotionally depleted and unsure how to proceed. One thing he did know, was that things would never be the same again, but he had love in his life. And forgiveness. That's all that mattered right now.

"Yes, dad. I'd like that very much."

Chapter 29

Adah found there would be some political backlash, as both Terrence Reed's grandfather and his Pastor had some serious community and political pull. She'd been asked several times—ordered, in fact—to make this case go away. Her career could stall if she didn't play ball. One case.

But how could she tank it when two women had their lives torn apart by a man who was callous, insensitive, and selfish? He'd gotten away with it because no one would hear Brittany's voice. But Adah heard it when she learned the previous detective on the case retired suddenly. She had her team pull financials and found a lump sum deposited into the man's account. No need to figure out where it came from and why. If she started picking which cases needed to go the distance, based on the old boy's network that was still in play, nearly half of these would fail before they even started. She could not be that woman.

Adah stood behind the mirrored wall watching Brittany Weaver as she entered the interrogation room. She also noticed Jacobson watching her and the front slit on her black skirt that showed off a pair of toned legs that held up a figure which caused most of the men to stare. "Ms. Weaver, please have a seat," Jacobson motioned.

Winship watched Jacobson taking in her entire form and nudged him forward, causing Jacobson to stumble into her. "I'm so sorry. Please have a seat."

Jacobson recovered while glaring at Winship, who grinned as he gestured to the chair.

"I'll see if the DA is ready." Winship strutted out of the room, chuckling.

Jacobson shuffled a few papers to hide his nervousness. "Did you rest well last night?"

"I did, thank you for asking," she said, oblivious to his angst and the fact that he was trying to hide his growing attraction to her.

She pushed a loose strand of hair behind her ear. "Do you think it'll be much longer?"

Adah Osmani left the viewing room and entered the interrogation room next door. Sticking her hand out to Brittany, she said, "I'm sorry to have kept you waiting Ms. Weaver."

Rising from the chair, Brittany shook Adah's hand as the DA's smile welcomed her.

"If you would follow me this way."

* * *

Brittany thought for sure they would remain in the interrogation room, but instead she went into Adah's quaint but immaculate office. From the picture on the desk, Ms. Osmani had two beautiful kids, but there was no man in the photo. Adah followed Brittany's line of sight to the family photo. "How was your drive?"

Tearing her eyes away from the image, she said, "It was uneventful, which is a good thing. I hate traffic."

"I understand you have a son as well. How old is he?" Adah inquired.

"He's nine. Let me show you his picture," she said reaching in her purse.

Adah scanned the photo, and it confirmed what the detectives had told her a few days ago. "May I ask who his father is?"

Brittany replaced the photo in a plastic sleeve within her wallet. "I'm sure you already know the answer to that."

Adah locked her fingers in front of her. "Does he know?"

"I haven't spoken to Terrence since I left school," Brittany said as she crossed her legs. "He didn't know that I was pregnant when I left. I didn't know either. I went home for the summer and never returned because what I thought was a stomach virus turned out to be an eight pound six-ounce baby."

Adah rubbed her forehead as she felt a serious headache coming on. Now that the press was interested in the case, it was becoming more of a bother and she'd be under more pressure to win or lose, if the powers that be had their way.

"We met on campus. He approached me for a date in the cafeteria. I thought he was kind of cute, but I wasn't ready to date anyone, especially someone I just met. He pursued me a while and called during Christmas break before I finally agreed to go on a date."

"Did you become intimate with him at that point?" Adah questioned.

"No, we dated for four more months and things were going great. The last month of school, things kind of changed. I'd already told Terrence that I was saving myself for marriage. He kept pushing the issue of us being intimate, but I stayed true to my word. Two weeks before we left for summer break, Terrence invited me over to his dorm room. We kissed and fooled around a little bit. He got a rise and wouldn't take no for an answer. I told him I wanted to leave, but he said I couldn't leave him like that, and he raped me."

The tears she should've shed nine years ago, but never had a chance to, finally made their presence known.

Adah handed Brittany some tissues and a bottle of water from her mini-fridge. "We'll take a moment before we continue."

After several minutes, Adah carefully waked the young woman through the testimony, trying to poke holes in Brittany's story. Her version of events did not change, which gave Adah more confidence. Once she was sure there was nothing left to cover, she said, "Great job. Monday we will do this for real."

Chapter 30

Adah looked at the six women and six men that made up the jury panel, evenly picked to hopefully avoid an acquittal. She felt sorry for Terrence because it looked as if his attorney, Greg Wallace, hadn't shown up. He probably had a better chance with the public defender, anyway. She glanced at her watch before taking her seat. Greg was tardy, and that certainly wasn't a good look for a man trying to gain back his status.

"All rise." The Honorable Kathleen Graham presiding." Bailiff Brown's voice echoed throughout the room that was filled to capacity.

"Be seated. Is the prosecution ready to proceed?" Judge Graham asked while flipping through the file.

"Your Honor." A man in a silver suit sauntered in toward the defense table. "Mr. Wallace was hit by a car last night and is in the ICU."

Gasps echoed, mirroring Adah's shock.

"It looks like we will have to postpone the trial," Judge Graham said.

"Oh no, Your honor. I can proceed with the case in his stead. I'm fully up to speed with everything, as I've been helping behind the scenes."

"Ms. Osmani, do you wish to postpone or proceed? Your call."

Adah scrutinized Khalid Saeed Hassan, her nemesis from law school. He was still as handsome as he was back then. The fact that he said he'd been helping all along was probably cause for alarm. Someone was footing the bill because Khalid didn't come cheap. She should know, he was also her husband at one point in time.

"We'll proceed, Your Honor." Adah's smile widened, and she went back to the prosecutor's table where her two paralegals awaited to assist with presenting her arguments. More delays meant witnesses became restless and lost even more faith in the system. She could be no more prepared than she already was, and postponing would only draw things out and line her ex-husband's pockets. Determined not to let Khalid unnerve her, Adah addressed the jury. "Ladies and gentlemen of the jury, the State will prove to you that the defendant raped his wife, causing bodily injury and a visit to the emergency room. What was supposed to be a romantic anniversary weekend turned into the worst night of Mrs. Reed's life. The State will also show this wasn't his first time not heeding a woman's right to say no."

Whispers went through the crowd, just as Percy entered the court room, taking a seat directly behind Hassan. After Adah finished her opening statement, she returned to her seat.

Hassan stood, squaring his shoulders, relishing the appreciative looks sent his way as he addressed the jury. "Your Honor, while the prosecution will have you believe that the defendant is a rapist, we'll prove that this was all a big misunderstanding. My client is just a man who was trying to explore something more than their normal sex life. Everyone can understand that." Khalid walked to the jury box before completing his address. "Things may have gotten just a little out of control, but the defendant was only trying to add some spice to their marriage by trying new things in the bedroom." Hassan gave Adah a lingering look, which she dismissed by putting her attention on the jury. "And he made a mistake. Just a mistake. Once we lay out the facts of the case, we'll prove beyond a reasonable doubt that he's a loyal friend, a faithful husband, an excellent father, and nothing like the prosecution is making him out to be."

"The prosecution can call their first witness," Honorable Judge Graham stated.

"The State calls Margaret Harper to the stand."

Margaret walked to the stand, her steps not quite as spry as Adah remembered. After being sworn in, she took her seat.

"Would you please state your name and occupation for the record?" Adah asked.

Margaret leaned forward toward the microphone, "My name is Margaret Harper and I'm the owner of Cedar Crest Bed and Breakfast."

Adah moved from her spot near the jury box to block Hassan from Margaret's view. She would not allow him to intimidate her witness, as Mrs. Harper was well aware that he had been the one to torment Adah for a number of years before she found her way to freedom. "Please describe for the court what you were doing on the night in question."

Margaret walked the court through a dinner date and her late-night cup of tea with her husband. She recounted Casey's disheveled appearance and being in shock as she came down the stairs. She also recounted how she feared for Casey's safety and insisted that she drive her to the hospital.

Adah purposely stepped in front of the witness stand, turned and pointed at Terrence while asking her next question. "Did the defendant at any time come down to assist his wife?"

"No, he didn't. I actually sent Roy up to their room because I was concerned, he might have been hurt as well," Margaret explained.

"Thank you, Mrs. Harper. No more questions," Adah said as she returned to her chair.

"Mrs. Harper," Hassan said, getting to his feet. "On the night in question, did you hear any screams coming from the defendant's suite?" Margaret's head whipped toward Adah. "No, but—"

"Just yes or no," Hassan insisted.

"No," Margaret replied, her shoulders relaxed.

"You say Mrs. Reed came down the stairs in her comforter, and you automatically assumed she'd been raped."

"Well, I know—"

"Yes or no," Hassan demanded.

"Yes," Margaret said in a hushed tone.

Hassan stood directly in front of Margaret with one hand in his pocket. With a smirk he asked, "Did it ever occur to you that there were no screams, so she must have liked what her husband had done?"

"Objection," Adah said, getting to her feet. "Calls for speculation."

"Sustained," the judge replied.

Hassan circled in front of the jury box. "You know how women get when it's good to them. They want to tell the whole world." "Objection," Adah jumped from her seat—again.

"Sustained," Judge Graham snapped, giving the defense attorney a warning glare. "Counselor, watch yourself."

Hassan squared his shoulders. "One more question. Did any guests or staff complain of noise?" "No."

"Thank you. No further questions," he said and gave Adah a side eye.

"The witness may step down," the judge stated.

"The State calls Olivia Whitaker to the stand."

After Olivia was sworn in by the bailiff, Adah approached the witness stand. "Please state your name and profession for the court."

"Olivia Whitaker. I'm a Sexual Assault Nurse Examiner or SANE Nurse. I'm part of a response team that assists victims of sexual assault. I perform the forensic exams."

Adah scanned the jurors' faces for acknowledgement of the profession.

"Olivia, how did you first come in contact with Mrs. Reed?"

"She came into the emergency room wrapped in nothing more than a white comforter and in her bare feet. I was assessing another patient at the time. By the time she filled out the paperwork, I was finished."

Adah paced in front of the witness box. "Can you describe for the court Mrs. Reed's demeanor on that day?"

"Objection. This calls for speculation," Hassan replied from the defense chair as he jotted down a few notes.

"Overruled. The witness will answer," came from the judge's bench.

"She was visibly upset, and she couldn't sit on any of the chairs. She even stood to fill out her paperwork."

Walking back to the wooden table, Adah accepted a picture from one of her paralegals. "Can you describe the injuries she sustained?"

Again, Hassan protested. "Objection, Your Honor. She's a nurse, not a treating physician."

"Denied," Judge Graham exclaimed. "She saw the injuries firsthand. Please answer the question, Ms. Whitaker."

"Mrs. Reed suffered internal and external sphincter tears," Olivia said as she shared a sympathetic look with Casey.

"Do you normally see these types of injuries in women who are in a loving relationship with their spouses?"

"No, we typically see them in assault victims."

Murmurs rippled through the room. Adah heard a comment float through the air from an older woman in the courtroom. "Mmmm, yep he's guilty." She almost smiled because those words reached the jury.

"One final question," Adah stated. "Did Mrs. Reed identify the person that violated her?"

"Yes, I said I hope they found the monster that violated her. She said, 'they don't have to look very far, he's my husband'."

Hassan said, "No questions at this time, but I reserve the right to recall the witness."

"How much later?" Mrs. Whitaker snapped, frowning. "I have a job. I need to be there for people when men like your client don't know how to act."

"Objection," Hassan growled, tossing his hands in the air.

"Sustained." The judge turned a disapproving eye toward the witness. "Outbursts like that taint the jury. The jury will disregard."

"On second thought, we won't be calling her again." Hassan glared at Adah, who wanted to run and give the feisty nurse a high-five.

"Thank you," Adah said and turned her attention to the front of the court room.

"The witness may step down," Judge Graham said.

After court adjourned for the day, Adah spoke with Brittany in the hall. "Tomorrow will be the pivotal part of the trial. I'll call you to the stand."

"Will the defense team try and trip me up like they did everyone today?" Brittany asked.

"I'm sure Attorney Hassan will try, but as long as you tell the court everything you've told me, you'll be fine. Besides your story hasn't wavered since I met you," Adah told her. "Keep it simple. Yes or No. Don't try to over explain."

After Brittany left the building, Adah went to the room where Casey was waiting.

Casey was still on the fence about testifying against Terrence. After asking how she was and reassuring her she'd be okay, Adah said, "You'll be my last witness. While I think your testimony will be the hardest because your emotional wounds are still fresh, I do believe you'll persevere. If you get frazzled, just think about those beautiful babies you have. I need you to go home and rest."

Chapter 31

Adah sat in her office going over case notes. The money trails were quite incriminatory. From the investigation into the previous detective's bank accounts, Adah uncovered a large deposit before he suddenly disappeared. Based on the statements from Percy Reed's account, the exact amount was removed from his bank the same day the counter deposit was made into the account of Detective Billy Hammonds. Five other large withdrawals from this same account and she would bet when she received statements from Brittany's bank, the transactions would match to the penny. Percy had been busy, but what was he trying to hide? Were there other crimes Terrence had committed that his grandfather had covered up, or were these Percy's crimes?

The sliding of feet across the wood floor caused Adah to reach in her desk for her nine-millimeter gun. It was very late. As far as she knew, she was alone in the building. She got to her feet but felt Khalid's presence before he ever crossed the threshold. No one else made the hairs on the back of her neck stand up. She placed the gun in the back waistband of her pants and prayed she wouldn't have to use it tonight. Khalid entered her office without knocking. On that alone, she should've kicked him out. His arrogance led him to believe there was no consequences for his actions.

"I didn't startle you, did I?" Khalid smirked.

Adah took two steps back just before he could touch her. "No, Khalid, you didn't. I smelled your cheap cologne before you made it in here."

Khalid laughed one of those deep belly laughs. "Now you know I've never worn cheap cologne in my life. I assume you forgot we were meeting tonight to try to reach a settlement in the case?"

She motioned for Khalid to sit in the chair in front of her desk. Instead, he chose the supple leather sofa that occupied the left wall of her office overlooking downtown Asheville.

"You could've let me know you were helping Greg on the case," Adah said from her position behind her desk.

Khalid sat up on the sofa, looked her up and down, and motioned for her to come sit on his lap. "Actually, I couldn't, and you know that."

Adah moved from behind the desk and positioned where she'd have a good shot if that became necessary. "As you know, I can't do that." She took a seat in the leather chair facing him. At one time, she had truly loved this man. But he was an arrogant, selfish man, almost like Terrence Reed. The difference was that even though Terrence could have any woman he wanted, and probably get whatever he wanted, he felt he needed to take it, instead of waiting. Khalid, on the other hand, felt she should take his emotional and physical abuse in silence. Thanks to Mrs. Harper, Adah learned that she didn't have to suffer that way.

"Are you ever going to forgive me?" Khalid slid to the edge of the sofa and she tensed.

Adah inched back toward her desk. "I forgave you a long time ago, Khalid. I just know my worth now."

"You knew who you were then and how valuable you were. I just didn't. But now I do." Khalid moved closer, stroked the side of her face. "I'll see you in court tomorrow."

"Who's bankrolling Terrance's defense? Are those same people paying for you, or did you turn to your own shady connections?" Adah asked as she stood and returned her chair to its rightful place.

Khalid stood. "They pay me for both, actually."

He stepped closer to her, tried to kiss her lips. She moved just out of his reach. Disappointment flickered on his face. "I still love you. Even if you don't believe that." He gestured to the hallway. "I'll walk you to your car."

Adah gathered her things and walked ahead of Khalid on wobbly legs. Why did this man still get to her?

* * *

"All rise. The Honorable Katherine Graham presiding," the bailiff proclaimed.

"Please call your witness."

"The state calls Brittany Weaver to the stand."

Adah glanced at the defense to gauge their reaction.

Terrence frowned, then leaned to whisper in Khalid's ear. He returned to an upright position as his parents took a seat behind him, with his father placing a reassuring pat on his shoulder.

"Your Honor, I haven't had time to research this witness," Khalid said as he walked toward the bench.

"Mr. Hassan, sit down."

"May we approach the bench, Your Honor?"

"No, you may not," she said, dismissing him with a hard look. "Ms. Osmani, continue please."

Adah approached the bench "Please state your relationship to the defendant."

"I was his girlfriend in college."

Adah looked down at her notes "How long did you date?"

"About nine months."

"Would you describe for the court what happened in your last month of dating?"

Brittany scanned the courtroom and her eyes locked with Terrence. Then she trained her eyes on Casey, staring at her while relating every detail of her relationship with Terrence — all with constant objections from the defense that only served to irritate the judge.

"Your Honor, once again, this testimony is irrelevant to the case," Hassan protested from his seat. "And it's wasting the court's valuable time."

"If the court allows, I will show how it is relevant," Adah offered.

"Continue please," Judge Graham replied, waving Hassan back into his chair.

"What happened after the defendant raped you?"

"Objection!" Hassan was on his feet again. "There's no police record of any kind that my client was involved in a rape." "Watch it, counselor," the judge warned Adah.

"Withdrawn. Did you consent to having sex with Mr. Reed?"

"Objection! Same line of questioning, Your Honor. Just worded differently. My client asserts he never had sex with that woman."

"Sustained." The judge arched a warning eyebrow.

Adah revised her line of questioning by leading in with, "So you ... dated him, then left school all of a sudden ..."

"Object--

"Sit down, Mr. Hassan."

Khalid plopped down in his chair, scowling.

"Did he try contacting you?"

"He never contacted me after that night. I wouldn't have wanted him to anyway. He ..."

"Yes, I know, but you can't say that here. There's no police record of it."

"There should be. I tried to press charges, but the detective stalled then disappeared altogether."

"Your Honor."

Judge Graham mulled that over for a second. "Counselor, limit your witness to testifying to things that are relevant to this case."

"Can you please tell the court what happened several months later?"

"I gave birth to a boy. I named him Tyler James."

"The state offers exhibit B into evidence," Adah said when the picture of Tyler James was pulled up on the screen.

Terrence flinched and blinked several times. Casey gasped, shot to her feet, and ran from the court room.

"But he claims that he never had sex with you."

The banging of the gavel sounded unreasonably loud as the judge tried to quiet the spectators. Adah watched Terrence's countenance register first shock, then despair when Casey stormed out of the court room. Evidently, he still held out a little hope that he could mend his broken marriage.

"The witness may step down."

"Your Honor, the defense requests a fifteen-minute recess," Hassan said.

"Permission granted."

Adah found Casey in the ladies' room crying. "I know this was a shock, and I couldn't prepare you for this but ..."

Casey blew her nose and tossed the tissue in the trash. "I'm fine. This just caught me by surprise. How did Terrence not know that he had a nine-year-old son?"

Adah placed her hand on Casey's back. "From the look on his face and his parents' faces, it was a shock to all of them. But did you notice who wasn't shocked?"

Casey frowned, tears drying as she came up with the answer. "Percy."

* * *

After the brief recess, the trial resumed. Adah was fully prepared to call what she believed was her last witness, but she switched gears and wanted to fill in the gaps of the testimony with another witness who was on the list, but the prosecution had glossed over all this time.

"The State would like to call Percy Reed to the stand."

All of the people at the defense table turned to look at Adah as if she'd lost her mind. Everyone in town knew Percy Reed.

"Objection, relevance?" Khalid quickly asserted. "The prosecution never stated they were going to call him as a witness."

"But he is on the list, Your Honor," Adah defended. "The State will show relevance once he's on the stand."

"Please proceed," the judge commanded.

Percy stood at his full height and walked with the gait of a more youthful man.

"Mr. Reed, I only have a few questions for you," she said walking to stand in front of him. "Please state your relationship to the defendant."

"He's my grandson," Percy replied, his chin lifted as he glared at Adah.

"Did you know that Terrence had a son by Ms. Weaver? And I will caution you that you are under oath."

"Yes, I knew about him," Percy stated, then shrugged. "What of it?"

Adah extracted the bank records from the prosecution table and slid them toward Percy. "Please tell the court exactly how you handled this issue so your grandson could remain in school."

Percy mumbled under his breath before saying, "I paid the detective six thousand dollars to make the police report disappear and placed a call to his commanding officer to have him called back into active duty."

Terrence's profanity-laced diatribe brought the judge up short and slamming the gavel to bring order to the court.

"What else, Mr. Reed?" she challenged, flipping to the last documents in the folder. "I mean, if you're going that far, you might as well go all the way."

"Objection," Khalid said. "The prosecution is testifying."

"Sustained."

"I also paid Ms. Weaver thirty thousand dollars and a monthly stipend to stay quiet about the kid," he snarled. "Which she did until you started meddling. Terrence didn't need to know about that boy. I was taking care of him. Her too."

Adah shifted her gaze to Terrence, who looked at his grandfather like he never knew the man. "Again, you ruined my life," he mouthed to Percy.

"Your Honor, in light of this evidence, I move that Percy Reed be taken into custody for evidence tampering and bribery," Adah suggested.

"You're reaching, Counselor," the judge warned. "You'll have to bring proper charges for that one."

"And that's my cue to leave," Percy said, tipping out of the witness stand and up the aisle.

Several people in the courtroom that had run-ins with Percy applauded as he damn near sprinted down the path to the door.

With that business out of the way, Adah shifted her gaze to Casey, whose face was nearly devoid of all color.

"The State would like to call Mrs. Casey Reed to the stand."

Shoulders squared, Casey sat in the witness stand. She gazed at Terrence, who had the nerve to look ashamed.

"Can you walk us through what happened on the night of February 10th?" Adah paced in front of the jury box, waiting for the response.

Casey relayed the events prior to arriving at the inn, their plans for a romantic evening, Terrence's assault, the visit to the emergency room, and leaving the inn. She even provided a taste of how life had been since they returned home. During her testimony, the jury panel's expressions ranged from sorrow, to anger, concern, and then downright rage.

"Your witness, Counselor," Adah stated as she walked to her seat.

Khalid approached the bench and smiled at Casey. "Mrs. Reed, we've heard your testimony. Did you scream for help when any of this happened?"

"Yes, I screamed several times for him to stop. I told him this was not something I wanted."

"Could you have misinterpreted his lovemaking because you were already mad at him?"

"Absolutely not." She shifted, trying to contain her anger.

"Are you sure this is not a dramatic way for you to get out of your marriage because you're unhappy?" Khalid asked as he walked back to the table and picked up a photo.

"No, that's not true," Casey snapped.

"In fact, isn't it true that you've been spending time with your partner Alexander Baxter?" Khalid questioned, and his tone left no doubt as to what he meant by "spending time".

"Objection," Adah said.

"Overruled."

Shock registered on Casey's face. Adah was well aware that Khalid could hit below the belt, but even she knew he was reaching on this one. Adah's team had done their own research and Casey came up clean in this regard.

"Yes, he is my partner, as well as my friend. It's not what you're implying," Casey protested.

"No further questions," Hassan said, but his smirk spoke volumes.

"Redirect, Your Honor," Adah asked.

Judge Graham nodded in Osmani's direction as she approached.

"Mrs. Reed, please tell the court why you were angry with the defendant that night."

"Because he was late picking me up. This made us late for our arrival at the inn. We spent an extra two hours in traffic when we could've been there already."

"In your opinion, was your husband just trying something new when he was ... as he calls it ... making love to you?"

"Objection. Calls for speculation."

"Overruled. Counselor, you're wearing it out."

With tears streaming down her cheeks, Casey said, "Loving doesn't require stitches, a full round of antibiotics and a consistent dose of pain meds."

Murmurs rippled through the courtroom.

Adah's tone was sober when she said, "No further questions."

Khalid and Terrence huddled together. After a moment, Khalid spoke "Your Honor, permission to approach please?"

"Very well."

"In light of this information and to save his wife and family further embarrassment, my client would like to change his plea to guilty. His only request is a chance to speak with both women before he is sentenced."

Adah glanced at Brittany and then Casey and said, "I'll see if they're up to it."

Chapter 32

Casey and Marla walked away from the courtroom for the last time. For Casey, the last year and a half of her life had been a nightmare. From the rape case, the separation, and the assault at the house that night, Terrence had sent their lives on a downward spiral.

"I can't believe he got fourteen years," Casey said. "I thought he'd be given a lot less time. The kids will be close to grown when he gets out."

Marla wrapped her arm around her friend. "There was enough evidence and testimony for the jury to find him guilty and for the judge to sentence him longer, if he hadn't pled guilty. Would've been more like twenty-five."

Casey laid her head on Marla's shoulder. "I should be relieved this is over, but now I have to explain to the kids that it'll be a while before they see their father again. I also have to break the news to them that they have a brother."

"Honey, kids are resilient. They bounce back quicker than adults. TJ is too young to even understand. Skye's a very bright girl and I'm sure if you explain things to her, she'll be fine. Don't sugarcoat it because she'll call you out on dumbing stuff down. You and the kids will be fine and I'm right here to help you through it."

Marla lifted Casey's head and stared in her eyes. "Besides, I believe a certain friend of yours will be here to help you get over Terrence as well." With a finger under her chin she nodded to the right where Alex stood waiting.

Glancing in his direction, Casey acknowledged him and gave a tiny smile that he would have missed if he'd blinked.

"I guess I should go and say something to him. I care for Alex a lot, but the only bandwidth I have right now is for my kids."

"Casey, nobody's saying you have to walk down the aisle with the man. Baby steps. Just talk to him."

Rolling her eyes at her friend, she said, "I'll be right back."

Casey walked toward Alex, with a little more energy in her step than she felt. Not as a woman who'd been broken by her storm, but as one full of strength and determination.

"Alex, thanks, I appreciate you coming to the trial," she said, reaching for his hand.

"You're more than welcome, but I wouldn't be anywhere else but right here. You should know that by now."

"Look, I…"

"Casey, go home and be with your kids. We can talk later." He kissed her cheek and walked away. He looked over his shoulder to find her watching him and smiled. She smiled back.

As she returned to where Marla stood, Casey placed a hand on her cheek, as if she were sealing the kiss in her skin before speaking. "Let's go home."

"Uhm hello, what was that? You're a free woman now, and I know you love that man. Why are you going home alone?" Marla rolled her neck while she spoke, letting a little ghetto girl drama come through.

"Now is not the time. I must believe that if we survived without going there this long, we can last a little while longer. Right now, is about me and my babies, and getting our lives back." Casey hooked her arm with Marla's and moved them forward. "Let's get out of here. I need to see my kids."

The ride home was peaceful, with both women enjoying the jazz music and each other's company. Casey swung by her mom's house to pick up

Skye and TJ. Things were mellowing out between them and for that, Casey was thankful.

Once she entered the house, TJ was the first to notice her. He ran over to her, arms outstretched, and dried mashed potatoes on his jaw.

"Hi, Mommy," Skye said as she wiped her brother's face with a paper towel.

"Hi, my big girl. Did you have fun with Grandma?"

"We always have fun here, especially when TJ plays with his food." Skye snickered showing the open spaces from her missing teeth.

Ella entered from the kitchen with a damp cloth, wiping the white substance from her hair as Casey tried to hide her laughter. To see her prim, proper mom's hair this way was too funny, and the humor in the situation won. She laughed the hardest she had in a year, as if the burdens from the earlier years were finally lifted from her shoulders and she was free.

Her mom was clearly not amused by her present state, but Marla certainly was. "That's it. Get it all out of your system," her mother warned.

Eventually, she also gave way to a fit of giggles that had taken over all of them. Before long, mother and daughter were in each other's arms on the floor crying, with a kid in each of their arms.

"Mom, I'm sorry again for what I said. I had no right to speak to you like that."

"Hush, girl. You already apologized once, and that was enough. I should've supported you and believed in you. I'm sorry. I'm glad you won your case."

"Thanks, Mom," Casey said as both tried to compose themselves.

Casey shifted to her knees, crawling as she gathered their toys. "Mom, I want to take them home and explain everything to them."

"Don't be surprised if you get more than you think from that one," her mom cautioned, pointing at Skye, who ran down the hall to the guest bedroom.

"Apparently some of her classmates were teasing her about her father being in jail today, but your daughter is smart and handled herself very well."

"Thanks Mom, I love you."

"I love you, too. Let me help you with the kids."

Casey made it home and sat with the kids, telling them as much as she felt they needed to know. Just as Marla and her mom said, Skye had an understanding that surpassed her age. The vacant space that Terrence left in their lives would be filled with the support of family and friends, and even his parents, who tried to make sure to pitch in where they could.

Happiness was within Casey's reach and she was all the better knowing that she deserved that and more.

Chapter 33

One Year Later

Casey's life was finally where she wanted. Her mom and Marla got her through more than a few terrible nights. Her practice was doing well, the kids were thriving with all of the attention from both sets of grandparents. In fact, Skye's academic performance meant she was able to skip a grade. TJ was becoming more adjusted to life without Terrence, but at times he would stare at the front door as though waiting for him to return.

She sold the old house and put some money in an account for Terrence when he was released. In the event he didn't make it out, the money would revert to the kids. Casey walked into Not Just Coffee for a caramel macchiato and a yogurt parfait. She checked emails on her phone as she waited. She heard the shuffling of feet and assumed the others had moved up. She stepped forward into a solid wall of muscles. "I'm so sorry, sir."

Consumed with an email she continued reading. As the line moved again, she bumped into the same wall and this time she looked up at the same time the man turned around.

"Casey." That velvety voice rolled over her like butter on a warm bun.

"Alex, I'm so sorry. What are you doing here? I've been coming in this place for a month and I've never seen you."

"Irene actually told me about it. She said the coffee was excellent, and the food wasn't bad either. How have you been? How's your new practice going?"

Casey noticed all the people in line around them listening to their conversation. "It's doing well. Let's get our orders and step outside. Folks are so nosey."

Alex got his breakfast and drink first and paid for hers as well. As they walked outside, he held the door.

"I'm going to step out on a limb here. Can we go to dinner tomorrow and catch up? I'll understand if you don't want to," he said, staring into her eyes, his own alight with expectation.

"That's perfect. I was going to suggest that myself." She placed a hand on his arm, saying, "I'm sorry I didn't stay in touch. I wanted to, but I needed to fix me first."

"I can understand that." Alex looked like he could skip down the yellow brick road from the Wizard of Oz. "I look forward to meeting the new and improved Casey."

"So, do I Alex," she whispered, smiling up at him. "So, do I."

Anita L. Roseboro-Wade, a native of North Carolina, has served as a Guardian Ad-Litem and Volunteer for a Rape Crisis Center. She pens poetry, articles, and stories that are centered around women's issues and thought-provoking subjects. Her work was recently published poetry in *The Heart Songs, a Poets and Writers Collective* edited by National Bestselling Author, Deborah Mello, and *Sugar an Anthology* with NK's Tribe Called Success featuring New York times Bestselling author, S.L. Jennings.

Born to parents who never finished high school, Anita has always understood the importance of education. She obtained a degree in MIS (Management Information Systems) and a Master's in Business Administration from Gardner-Webb University and the University of Phoenix respectively. She is a devoted mother, caregiver, and is currently working on her next novel, A Father's Fall from Grace. Visit her on the web www.anitalroseboro.com

Summer Breeze

Anita L. Roseboro

About *Sweet Summer Breeze*

Summer is still mending a broken heart from a relationship that ended long before its expiration date. When she runs into her ex, Devon, he tells her the most devastating news she's heard since her mother was murdered. Then she learns that a mysterious woman, with ties to Devon, is stalking her under the guise of becoming a client. Summer now has to figure out if she's been targeted as her mother had been.

Devon promised to love Summer forever. Unfortunately, forever came much too soon when she made it clear that they had different goals in life and love. After their breakup and a few drinks, he finds himself engaged and soon to be a father with a woman he barely knows. The more Summer and Devon fight their feelings for each other while they uncover the truth behind the mysterious situations that occur, the more they are drawn together. Now with new developments that are not in his control, he must face Summer and risk breaking her heart again, while figuring out the secrets that his new wife is keeping.

Karen has infiltrated Summer's life, trying to right old wrongs. She will do anything to save the child she carries, even sacrifice herself to put it in the hands of a woman who will protect it from a man who wants the child— and her—for his own lurid purposes. How long can she hide in plain sight, redeem herself in Summer's eyes, before all that is hidden comes to the light?

Devon and Summer are soon confronted with the fact that one woman holds the keys from a dangerous past and an even more devastating future.

Chapter 1

Sleep never came until first light. For almost ten years, Summer's nights had been spent tossing, turning, and chasing ghosts. The Blues joints in Atlanta were the only places where she felt at home. People went to places like that because they were running from one thing or another. Hiding from themselves and the ghosts within. Something she and they had in common.

Summer settled into the leather seat in a cozy corner of Café 290. The music unwound the coils of stress wrapped around her, that tried to squeeze what was left of any peace of mind. Being the Director of The Guardian Ad Litem office meant fielding daily calls from volunteers, social workers at their breaking points, and lawyers who'd become weary of the system. The turnover rate in her department was at an all-time high. Budget cuts from the state and the increased need to hire more volunteers put a strain on her reserve. Now, she simply needed relaxation. Slowly, she sipped a glass of "Black Bubbles" Sparkling Shiraz and let the melodious saxophone soothe her soul as the cares of her world slipped away.

A tall, slender man moved toward her. He had a familiar gait that signaled he was seeking out his next prey. Summer Daniels was no one's prey or victim.

"Hey, that seat for me?" he asked.

Summer looked up with a heated intensity that made good on her name. "I prefer to sit by myself, thank you."

"A pretty lady like yourself should never be alone," he said, in what he believed was a seductive tone.

"That wasn't an invitation for you to convince me. Have a good night."

The man glared at her, then slithered off, mumbling something that rhymed with witch. Normally, it took a few of these exchanges for the rest of the men to get the message. One night, the high count was twelve.

Summer slowly returned to her zone and closed her eyes to absorb the music.

"Who's playing tonight?"

The sound of his silky voice made Summer tremble unexpectedly. Places on her anatomy where he provided hours of pleasure long ago now reacted spontaneously. She lifted her gaze to meet those dark brown eyes.

"Maria Howell and Bill Wilson," she replied.

Café 290 was the last place she thought she'd run into the love of her life, the man who shattered her heart. During a more pleasant time in their relationship, she had believed they were destined for the 2.5 kids, white picket fence, and rocking chairs. Not to mention, they were all set to overhaul the overworked social and justice system. Somehow, neither dream materialized.

"You always loved those sparkling bubbles hitting your nose."

"And you always loved watching me make a fool of myself," she replied, allowing a smile to come.

She joined him in boisterous laughter.

"Never that. You let your guard down fighting those bubbles, and it was a beautiful thing to see," he said.

Devon snatched a chair from the table and situated it next to her. Evidently, he'd tired of waiting for her to extend the invitation. She had no intention of inviting heartbreak back into her life again. She was all good picking up the lesson on the first time out.

"How you been?" he asked.

"Wonderful," she lied, knowing full well that life had dealt her several blows. Some of them landed because he was no longer in her life. "What about you?"

"I'm good," he answered.

Boy, could she tell. The man looked delectable in a suit, but he was even hotter in a pair of jeans that fit his muscular frame.

"It seems life is treating you well," she said, her gaze roaming his body, reacquainting her mind with the best aspects of his physique— those powerful thighs, that gorgeous rear-end, six-pack, muscular chest and arms. His neck invited kisses, and so did those lips. "I haven't seen you around here since you ended things."

"I've got something important to tell you," he replied, his gaze lowering to the table where her purse rested.

"I've been getting over the loss. You tracked me down because you want to give us a second chance?"

Summer thought back to when they worked in the same office, but because of a "no fraternizing" clause, she walked away. The move seemed right at the time; his career was more established than hers. She thought making this ultimate sacrifice would solidify their relationship. Boy was she wrong.

"I'm waiting," she said, sliding closer as an up-and-coming musician took the stage while the duo took a break.

Somehow, he avoided giving out the good news as the two of them talked about parts of their past, the aspect of their relationship she missed the most.

"I'm getting married in two weeks. We're expecting a baby in December."

Chapter 2

He presented those two pieces of info and had the utter gall to smile the entire time, not realizing that the rest of her world had taken a plunge.

Summer nearly choked on her drink. The liquid slid down the wrong pipe and she coughed to clear her airways. Devon slid the drink from her hand and gave her a few pats on the back to help things along. Once she regained her composure, she could barely wrap her mouth around saying anything.

"I'm happy for you." Infuriated was a better word. How could he marry someone else in such a short amount of time, when he had professed that he'd love Summer forever?

On the real, she had no one to blame for this but herself. She lost him because of her unwillingness to commit, but she had a good reason. Even if he still didn't believe a word of it.

"I remember a time when you didn't want a child," Summer said, schooling her facial expression to stay neutral.

"I wanted one, but you didn't want to be married. Why would you carry my seed and not be my wife? Most women want things in reverse," Devon countered, locking his fingers into a teepee with his index finger under his chin.

"Wow. Really?" She said, feeling every bit of the censure in his tone. "So, explain how your fiancé is expecting. Did you ask her to marry you before or after the baby came along?" She glared at him, watching his mouth part and then close.

His expression hardened.

"For the record, I had no problem with either one. The timing was wrong."

She grabbed her purse and stood but paused as she felt his touch. "I'll catch you some other time," she said, shrugging him off.

"Please stay," he whispered, standing so they were eye to eye. "I wanted to tell you before anyone else did."

"You succeeded."

Chapter 3

"I ran into an old friend tonight at Cafe 290," Devon announced as he slid out of his black jeans and white shirt. He exchanged them for a pair of navy pajama bottoms.

"Surely, not Summer," Charity said, her tone as dry as her facial expression. The jealousy toward his ex-girlfriend ran deep, but he didn't understand it.

"She seemed different somehow," he replied, taking his place next to her on the bed. He slid the remote from the glass nightstand and flipped to CNN. "I barely mentioned that we're getting married and we're expecting."

Charity snuggled into him. "I'm sure that's the last thing she expected to hear."

"Maybe, but she needed to hear it from me, not some random person," he said, still pained by the expression on Summer's face as she rushed away. She even forgot to pay for her drinks.

"What difference does it make who she heard it from?" Charity snapped. "She's no longer your concern."

She rolled onto her side and placed her hand over her stomach.

"She'll always be my concern, regardless of our relationship," he countered. "This with you was a total surprise to me. I was honest about that."

She glared at him and rolled away. She was asleep before he could say anything else.

Devon's thoughts drifted to Summer as he watched Charity. Maybe if he'd been a little less demanding about having kids immediately after marriage, she would be the one sleeping next to him. He had been shocked at her stance on waiting three years after marriage to have kids. That was the issue. He knew if he didn't lock in the terms, she would find a way to extend them.

Despite his feelings for Charity and their unborn child, he still loved Summer. She would always be the love of his life, but Devon would do everything in his power to protect Charity from being hurt. He cared for her and wanted to provide for his child—if it was actually his child.

Charity had approached him at Sweet Georgia's Juke Joint a few months after his separation from Summer. That wasn't long enough to get over what he'd felt would be the love of a lifetime. At the time, his heart still being held hostage didn't matter to Charity.

How two drinks ended with a one-night stand was a puzzle he'd never figure out. He was still fuzzy on the details of their night together, when she swore their child was conceived. As a Que, he could drink his frat brothers under the table. So, how two drinks could put him so far out of the zone that he couldn't remember ending up at her house, let alone sleeping with her, was a mystery.

Chapter 4

Summer again spent the night wrestling with her pillows. The pain of finding out that Devon had moved on so quickly when she was still on the fringe of heartbreak was almost too much to bear. She tried to push that aside, but only snatched two hours of sleep.

All court cases were on Wednesday, which usually made for a hectic Thursday.

"Summer, did you have a late night?" asked her secretary Daryl Simmons, poking her head into Summer's office. "Would you like some coffee?"

"No, thanks. What's the first hearing for today?"

"Actually, all the hearings for today have been postponed," Daryl said as she entered the room with a bottle of water. "They haven't been able to find a replacement judge to sit in for Judge Waters." "What happened to him?" Summer asked.

"Food poisoning. He was admitted to Emory University Hospital late last night." Daryl placed the much-needed bottle of water on Summer's desk.

"Sounds serious. Probably from eating Marge's cooking again," Summer remarked with a laugh. The judge often joked that his wife's meatloaf would be the death of him.

"Maybe more of a precaution, since he had a hernia and the bleeding ulcer last year," Daryl replied. "You only have two appointments today: one at three and the other at five."

"I'll be in my office catching up on the research the clerk sent. Were you able to find out any more about the person coming in later?" Summer took a sip of her water, and wished it were coffee, one of the vices she'd given up a few months ago when missing one of the five cups in her day started bringing on headaches.

"Only that she's new in town, and somehow thinks she might need someone to help protect her child," Daryl replied as she swept out of the office.

As the evening drew near, Summer finished her call to a social worker concerning a wandering child who was found eating her neighbors' cat food. The child was immediately placed in Child Protective Services, and Summer arranged for a volunteer to meet with the child.

"Summer." Daryl knocked and entered the office simultaneously.

"Yes." Summer waved her in with the phone she was placing in its cradle."

"Oh, I'm sorry," Daryl said, pulling up a chair in front of Summer's desk. "I didn't mean to disturb you, but your five o'clock called and said she had an emergency. She'll call and reschedule."

"Did you find out any more about her?" Summer flicked her pen on the desk. If the woman had been more considerate, Summer could have left an hour ago.

"Only her first name, Charity. When I asked for her last name, she said it wasn't important," Daryl replied, her purple hued lips pulling into a smirk. "Why are you concerned about this one?"

Summer rubbed the stress from her neck. "The vibe I got the day we spoke gave me chills."

"Well, I've known you for five years, and I don't ever recall you being wrong about something feeling off. That's how you've landed such a good track record."

"If she calls back, try to reschedule her with someone else. I'm going to work out and then go home. Set the answering machine and take the afternoon off, since we have no appointments this afternoon. No sense in both of us missing out on this beautiful weather. I know you've been working some very late hours since we took on two other districts. Our caseload has tripled. Please call the temp agency tomorrow and get some additional help."

"Thanks, Summer. I could use a little help, now that you mention it."

"Get out of here and have a good night."

Summer left the gym, her mind filled with conversations with Devon. She didn't want to risk running into him again, so another visit to the jazz club was out. The maze of traffic seemed very thick for this time of day, so she dashed off I-75 to take a more scenic route home through one of the more affluent neighborhoods off Northside Drive. Something about looking at the beautifully landscaped yards reminded her of a happier time in life, when her parents were together.

Summer arrived at her two-story east lake Tudor home in a quiet DeKalb County neighborhood. The nearby golf course added to the serenity. She wanted nothing more than to take a hot bath and relax, so after finishing her meal, she allowed the soothing water to lull her into an unsettled sleep. Her cell phone rang in the middle of her torrid dream, interrupting Devon holding and loving her, right at the point he was to thrust inside her. She jolted awake and grabbed the phone. "Hello."

After a long pause, she heard a familiar voice. How could a dead woman be on the other end of the line?

Want more? Pick up your copy of *Summer Breeze*.

The story kept me on edge. A mystery that was suspenseful, iced with some spicy romance. It was like watching an episode of Law and Order.

Summer Breeze
One hot summer brings an unexpected blast from the past
National Bestselling Author
ANITA L. ROSEBORO

GRAPHICS WITH FINESSE

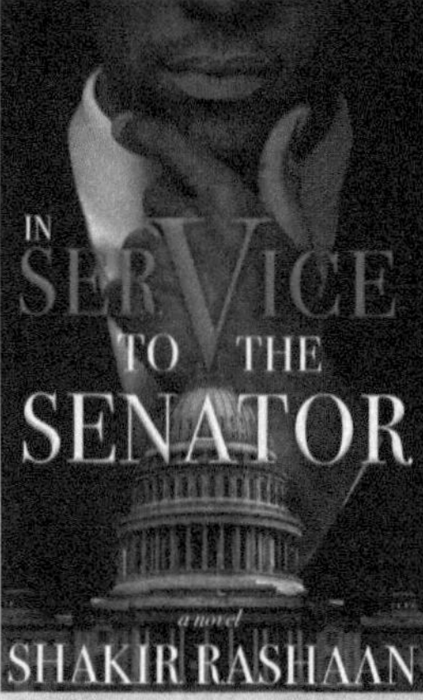

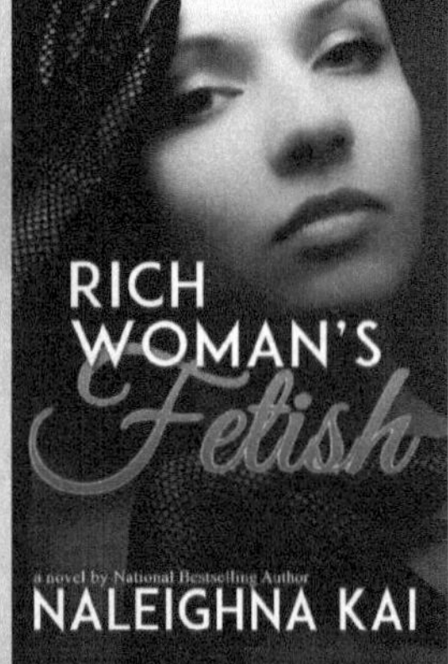

www.woodsoncreativestudio.com